Stories by Contemporary Writers from Shanghai

RIVER UNDER
THE EAVES

This book is edited and designed by the Editorial Committee of *Cultural China* series

Text by Yin Huifen
Translation by Zhu Jingwen
Cover Image by Chen Xidan
Interior Design by Xue Wenqing
Cover Design by Wang Wei

Assistant Editor: Cao Xiaoying
Editors: Wu Yuezhou, Anna Nguyen
Editorial Director: Zhang Yicong

Senior Consultants: Sun Yong, Wu Ying, Yang Xinci
Managing Director and Publisher: Wang Youbu

ISBN: 978-1-60220-253-5

Address any comments about *River under the Eaves* to:

Better Link Press
99 Park Ave
New York, NY 10016
USA

or

Shanghai Press and Publishing Development Company
F 7 Donghu Road, Shanghai, China (200031)
Email: comments_betterlinkpress@hotmail.com

Printed in China by Shenzhen Donnelley Printing Co., Ltd.

1   3   5   7   9   10   8   6   4   2

RIVER UNDER THE EAVES

By Yin Huifen
Translated by Zhu Jingwen

Better Link Press

Foreword

This collection of books for English readers consists of short stories and novellas published by writers based in Shanghai. Apart from a few who are immigrants to Shanghai, most of them were born in the city, from the latter part of the 1940s to the 1980s. Some of them had their works published in the late 1970s and the early 1980s; some gained recognition only in the 21st century. The older among them were the focus of the "To the Mountains and Villages" campaign in their youth, and as a result, lived and worked in the villages. The difficult paths of their lives had given them unique experiences and perspectives prior to their eventual return to Shanghai. They took up creative writing for different reasons but all share a creative urge and a love for writing. By profession, some of them are college professors, some literary editors, some directors of literary institutions, some freelance writers and some professional writers. From the individual styles of the authors and the art of their writings, readers can easily detect traces of the authors' own experiences in life, their interests, as well as their aesthetic values. Most of the works in this collection are still written in the realistic style that represents, in a painstakingly fashioned fictional world, the changes of the times in urban and rural life. Having grown up in a more open era, the younger writers have been spared the hardships experienced by their predecessors, and therefore seek greater freedom in their writing. Whatever category of writers they belong to, all of them have gained their rightful places in Chinese literary circles over the last forty years. Shanghai writers tend to favor urban narratives more than other genres of writing. Most of the works in this collection can be characterized as urban literature with Shanghai characteristics, but there are also exceptions.

Called the "Paris of the East," Shanghai was already an international metropolis in the 1920s and 30s. Being the center of China's economy, culture and literature at the time, it housed a majority of writers of importance in the history of modern Chinese literature. The list includes Lu Xun, Guo Moruo, Mao Dun and Ba Jin, who had all written and published prolifically in Shanghai. Now, with Shanghai re-emerging as a globalized metropolis, the Shanghai writers who have appeared on the literary scene in the last forty years all face new challenges and literary quests of the times. I am confident that some of the older writers will produce new masterpieces. As for the fledgling new generation of writers, we naturally expect them to go far in their long writing careers ahead of them. In due course, we will also introduce those writers who did not make it into this collection.

Wang Jiren
Series Editor

Contents

River under the Eaves   **9**

Jiqing Li   **97**

River under the Eaves

My family was an unusual one. It was filled with the spirit of freedom, romance and independence.

My grandma on my father's side was barely literate, but born in Shanghai and influenced by her businessman father. She learned to view this world with a free business spirit. She was straightforward, unrefined and folksy, and her lively language was always colored with folk adages. Even Huazi, a family member who received higher education and later married into high society, would go back to her uninhibited self, coloring her language with earthy slang that would have put high class society to shame. Dad in his youth was known for his good looks in the alleyway. In contrast to the simple alleyway, his tall stature and fancy clothing put him in the category of a Shanghai-styled dashing man. Dad was involved with another woman for six years, but Grandma never bad-mouthed him, and I never looked down on him either. Why? He was the one who made it possible for me to understand the world and enjoy freedom never allowed to other kids of my age. Soon after Mom ditched the family when I was 11, Dad had the femme fatale moved in. A decision both Grandma and I accepted without protest. I had been a reckless child when growing up. You might say that I wanted to cross the street before I learned to walk, and swear before I even learned to speak. Many people attributed that to my preternatural gift. I also believed that I would grow up to be a great person. By that time, I would say that I owed it all to my childhood and my family.

I came to know the word "dirty" at the early age of two.

I loved to be around my Aunt Huazi at that age. At the time, Huazi was still single even though she had past the usual marrying age. She wasn't tall, but was a real beauty with fair skin and soft to the touch body. Not at all like my skinny and tough skinned mother. Huazi also liked to have me around. She often held me in her arms and rolled in bed. She would even let me play "riding the bus" by sitting astride while shaking to mimic the bus movement and making the tooting sound. When nobody was around, she would even change her underwear in front of me. She apparently never took me for a man. One day, she locked the bathroom door behind her, I had no idea what she was doing in there.

"Let me in!" Pounding the door as I yelled from outside.

"Go away, dirty boy!" Huazi responded with a laugh. This was the first time I ever heard the term "dirty." I could sense that her laugh was different from her usual laugh, she was actually egging me on. I pounded even harder.

Later on, Huazi always related this detail to other family members. She said that I was already dirty and sexy at two. What she meant to say was that I already had an idea of what happened between men and women, and I seemed to have feelings for others.

As we celebrated the Chinese New Year at the house of Uncle Jianguo that same year, I had a real good time by getting myself exhausted by tumbling on the ground and running around. In the kitchen cluttered with fish, fowl and meat of all kinds, I found a narrow strip of flesh buried underneath a huge container of pork meat. I later found out that it was a pigtail. At that time, I thought it looked very much like my penis and I tried to get it out. When my cousin Xiaoli came walking by, I told her that I wanted the "penis." She giggled, much like the way Aunt Huazi giggled by covering her mouth and tittering vaguely. I also covered my mouth and laughed. Xiaoli ran to the living room in laughter and told everyone what I said. Then everyone in laughter came to the kitchen to see me. I was still standing there with a stupid smile on my face.

I have to add that Black Bug is one of my nicknames.

Many people in our alleyway had nicknames. Dad was given the nickname Stinky Bug because he was known for releasing smelly gases. And since he was a bug, I had to be a member of the bug's family, too. Our old neighbor Uncle Jin was nicknamed Shellac, a furniture varnish. He often showed up in cheap western suit, with his waxy hair glistening like a freshly varnished piece of furniture. Shellac and Dad went to the same elementary school, they had been friends since they wore open crotch pants. One of my classmates Beibei lived upstairs in my building. Her father was nicknamed Little Missy for his delicate features. He was in fact better looking than either Beibei or her mother.

There were all sorts of other monikers given to people in the alleyway, such as Torn Socks, Asshole, Old Clam, Light Bulb, Small Braid, and the Bride. They were all of roughly the same age as my Dad. Whereas the nicknames of my grandma's generation were much simpler, mostly referring to the places they came from many years ago, like Old Wuxi, Old Guangdong, Old Shandong, Old Suzhou. What is odd though was the nickname given to my now deceased Grandpa: "Little Wuxi." I just didn't get it, does it mean that he never grew old? I was also baffled by another nickname given to our neighbor who lived two doors away: "The Bride." Her daughter Jiajia was of the same age as I, how could she still be a bride?

I liked the nicknames from my Dad's generation because they were funny. They would bring a smile to your face every time. The funniest nickname belonged to the grandson of Old Shandong. Old Shandong was crazy about mahjong so when his daughter-in-law was pregnant he joked that they would be named after the mahjong tiles. If it was a boy, he would be named One Bamboo and if it was a girl, she would be named One Circle. Hearing this, all the players laughed their heads off. So his grandson was stuck with the nickname One Bamboo. As to why I was named Black Bug, I had my grandma to be thankful for. They say that when I was born my penis was a lot darker than the rest of my body. Grandma plucked it and said, "Just like a black bug!"

And I was known as the Black Bug from that day on. When I learned to cross the street and buy things from nearby stores, I became an errand boy for others. This gained me another nickname the Street Runner, or sometimes even Black Bug Street Runner. So I had two nicknames. I was different from the others.

At the age of three, I was able to cross the street on my own and wander about town. I also learned to buy things from stores and eat at small restaurants. I had been to all the nearby big streets and small lanes by myself. And I learned how to play mahjong.

The year when I turned three was also when mahjong made a comeback and became the most popular national pastime after disappearing for over 30 years. Mom and Dad learned the game fast and were addicted to it. They would play mahjong every day way past bed time. Grandma was an old pro in mahjong playing. She got busy finding mahjong partners, as if she had been rejuvenated by the game. She was physically in good shape at the time. Most of the time, Dad would play at home and Mom would play somewhere else. And I would stand by Dad and watch them play. That was how I learned the game. But I would start making noises and crying for attention when I got bored of the game.

"Go to bed!" Dad would shout at me still staring at his tiles. He wanted to get rid of me.

"No! I want to go to bed with you!"

"You are such a nuisance. Here, take two bucks and go get yourself something to eat at Asi's store across the street."

"Black Bug is too young. Stinky Bug, do you think it's safe for him to cross the street on his own?" said Shellac, who sat across the table from Dad. He looked at me while smoking a strange cigar. Shellac was very westernized.

"I have shown him how several times. There shouldn't be any problem," Dad responded casually.

I could see Shellac's well-oiled hair sparkling under the room light. Shellac's hair left a nice and deep impression on me from that day on.

I took the money and bought some yummy stuff at Asi's store across the street. I recklessly crossed the street. Several bicycle riders almost crashed while trying to avoid me, and one rider made a huge S turn and gracefully rode away. Asi's was a cigarette store. His parents were retired workers who helped out by stocking the place. That's why there was the good stuff that the other small stores didn't have.

After I learned to cross the street and buy things from Asi's store, Dad, the Bride, Old Shandong, Shellac, and all those who happened to sit around the mahjong table would often ask me to run errands for them. I'd buy cigarettes, matches or snacks, and get a reward after delivering the goods. Beibei, who lived upstairs, used my service when she received her allowance. She didn't dare to cross the street and would stay put on one side while I dashed across the street and ran back. My service was free for her. When I came back with the snack in my hand, the admiration and joy shown in her eyes would fill my heart with pleasure.

Sometimes I avoided Asi's store and went to a beautiful candy store at the corner for foreign candies, or even further to an unknown store several streets away. After a while, the clerks all knew me. They would immediately fetch me my favorite snacks the minute I walked in the door and before anything was said. Grandma said that the way I behaved myself reminded her of a city bum or fake fop of the old society.

Over time, my adventures went farther and farther away. Several times. I was cursed by drivers who had to hit the brakes in close calls, "You little devil!" I would throw a "Fuck you!" in return. I learned those alleyway swear words early in life.

I also liked the small wontons made by Old Shandong. He didn't have a business license, but every morning he would deliver the wontons he and his wife made to their customers. Waiting in the alleyway, I would see Old Shandong running from door-to-door.

In our household, lights would stay on late into the night every day, and I was used to that kind of life. I would never go to bed before midnight. I would slip out and play when Dad and Mom were "piling up the tiles." No one would notice my absence anyway. And when I came back covered in dirt, I would get some mumbled complaints at most. When they played past a meal time, they would often settle for cold leftovers before returning to their game. I sometimes had noodles accompanied by ribs with Dad at the store near the alleyway entrance.

By then, the whole idea of normal families having three meals a day became foreign to me.

What I loved the most was the summer time, when I filled myself with cold drinks every day. Dad later resigned from his old job and leased a place to start a business. He was doing very well for a while and his wallet was full of money. For snacks from Asi's store, I didn't have to use cash any more. With Dad's acquiescence I could run a tab there, and Asi would settle the account with Dad from time to time. Unfortunately, Asi was not a smart businessman. He usually would not let my tab run too high and would sometimes ask for my grandma's permission first. Grandma was always against me and would refuse to give her permission, of course. I would then raise hell against her. Usually, I would scream in protest at the top of my lungs. In return, Grandma would harshly scold me, but she couldn't do it for long. It didn't take too long before we were left gasping for air.

"You little devil! Do you want to kill me? Your childhood is going to determine the man you will become, you will grow up a gangster! Don't you touch my television!" she said. That TV was Grandma's love. It was a gift to her by Uncle Jianguo after he came back from Tanzania. Jianguo was a construction worker who had been sent to work on a housing project in Tanzania. Grandma said the television set was the fruit of his hard labor.

"I want cold drinks, ah ..." I flipped the TV knobs back and forth on purpose. The screen showed only snowflakes. I continued to howl in protest. My howling and screaming was quite famous in our alleyway by now.

"You had three ice creams and you still want more? You could have stomach problems by having too much of that stuff. And when you have problems, they will blame me. I have to tell your parents that if they don't discipline, then they shouldn't have kids. You are all rascals!" Covering her ears, Grandma dragged me away from the TV set and reset it to the original channel.

"You old scumbag. You are an old scumbag!" I said this in defiance.

"Are you calling me names? Did you learn it from your mother? Son of a bitch! Animal!" she screamed back at me.

I know that Grandma was actually scolding Mom.

Both Dad and Mom had had their fights with Grandma. One time, Dad stole Grandma's savings because he had stocking fees that were due. When she found out, she fought with Dad and asked him to return the money right away. Dad answered, "I don't have money, all I have is this life of mine!" With a threatening look on his face, Dad uttered those words in a low voice, and Grandma went mute. When I fought with Grandma, I chose to annoy her with loud shrieks, to which she could only cover her ears as a defense. Sometimes Asi would shake his head and leave the scene when our fighting escalated, and that was when Grandma called out for him.

"Asi, just give him the ice cream. Something other than chocolate ice cream. What else can I do?"

"I want chocolate ice cream! I want chocolate ice cream!"

"All right, all right. You debt collector! Alas, the world's practices are declining and the people have also changed for the worse. I might as well turn a blind eye to what is happening around me ..." Grandma would shake her head in resignation and turn to the TV. Her TV was always on.

I knew that Grandma doted on me. How dare I to scream

and shout at her, even verbally abuse her? Nobody ever told me this, but I knew that Grandma's curse words were meant for Mom and Dad.

At night, the Triangle Market was my favorite haunt. It was the largest market of Shanghai at the time. It was a building with a roof, but no walls, crowded with countless rows of counters. The smell of fish and green vegetables permeated the air. The weak light bulbs made the whole place seem enormously huge and endlessly long. I, like a small fish, would swim aimlessly inside, moving from place to place. Together with other wandering kids of the same kindred spirit and also the best of friends, such as Shellac's son Little Black Skin and One bamboo, the grandson of Old Shandong, we chased each other for fun. Unfortunately, these kids were not allowed to stay out too late. At night time, their mothers would watch them closely like a hen watching out for her little chicks. I would be left alone in the end. Beibei and Jiajia had followed me there and played, they shrieked because they found the place so exciting. My special counter-hopping skills were truly eye-opening. Of course, I missed a few times and got bruises all over my face. It was a pity that Beibei broke her shinbone when trying to follow my antics, and was confined to bed for a whole month. Since then, her father, Little Missy, would refuse to let her play with me outside anymore.

Little Missy was really not a likable person. He worked someplace as an accountant. With glasses and a clean intellectual look, he acted as if he had no intention of mixing it up with people like us. As a boy, he was particularly neat and would only spit in front of someone else's house, according to Grandma. The only thing that he did that deserved my admiration was bringing home unused spreadsheets from his work unit and using them as toilet paper and packaging paper. The sheets were white as snow and soft to the touch. Beibei and I used them to make airplanes and how those planes could fly.

I enjoyed my free time running around inside the market. I

was grateful to Mom and Dad who were engrossed with playing mahjong. It gave me freedom that the other kids would envy. Later, two chess-playing old men attracted my attention. They always made their entrance late into the night when it was quieter and with fewer people. Under the market light, they started playing chess on a small stools. They each carried a small Yixing teapot and moved the chess pieces impassively without a word. That aroused my curiosity. I waited for a long time for them to talk. They usually opened up after two games.

"Little devil, aren't you going home? This is strange, don't you have parents?"

And I would take the cue and run back home right away.

I spent the whole summer watching them playing chess every night, and learned the game without even trying. Once, I scored consecutive wins when playing casually chess with Shellac. Later on, I became the chess champion of the alleyway by beating everyone, including Dad and Light Bulb, the known best player of the alleyway. Dad was so flabbergasted, he kept on saying, "This little devil has some chess-playing talent. Who knows? He may turn out to be another legendary Chinese chess player like Hu Ronghua one day."

"You have a bright future ahead of you," said Dad, looking at me very seriously. I was surprised by his comment. It was the first time that I became someone important in his eyes.

To this day, I still don't know who Hu Ronghua is. In all seriousness, Dad found a chess teacher for me, and the teacher required me to play at least ten games a day. For about a month, I was inundated with all kinds of chess game plans. Sitting all the time caused my butt to bruise. I soon got bored. I felt that Dad's beautiful dream actually had nothing to do with me. And I had no intention to become that Hu Ronghua guy, who looked just awful in my imagination.

As I became bored with chess, Dad was hurtling head over heels into the "future" of an extra-marital affair. Busy in hot pursuit of that young girl, he had no time to worry about my future. Since I didn't care much about my so-called future, I continued my aimless wandering.

I knew our neighborhood like the palm of my hand through all the years of wandering. After a while, the neighbors all knew that I was their go-to person if they needed anything out of the ordinary.

"Black Bug, do you know where to find the electrical bar for electric tea kettles?"

"Black Bug, where to buy candles and tinfoil nearby?"

"Black Bug I would like to buy insoles ..."

I always had answers for their questions and even volunteered to serve as their guide. I was the one who led Beibei's grandma to buy coffin clothes at the side of the bridge on Sichuan Road. People started calling me the Street Runner. When I crossed the street at the speed of a lightning rod, the same people would be so scared that they would scream, "Watch out! Watch out! You scared me to death!"

"Black Bug, Street Runner, you come back, I don't want you as my guide anymore!"

I would burst out laughing from across the street. I believed that deep down they wanted me to be their guide and they weren't worried that I might get hit either. They were actually worried about their own heart conditions. That's when I became picky in doling out my help. I would give answers and only act as a guide for the people I liked, such as Shellac and Beibei. They would follow my moves closely instead of providing over-the-top reactions.

There was an old bicycle whose pedals I could barely reach lying around the house, and it soon became my toy. I ended up with super bicycling skills and the bike had also proven to be an enormous help in my future adventures.

Generally speaking, I liked women over men. Women would touch my head and hold conversations with me right by my side. Their hands were as soft as Mom's. Dad and Mom had been fighting for a divorce for six years, and Mom's attitude towards me during this time was mixed, sometimes affectionate and sometimes standoffish. Even the times she spoke to me, she never tried to hug or even get close to me. That was why I liked women over men. Mom moved out after the divorce, and that deepened my desire to be around women. I had no feeling for Mom. She rarely gave me money, she was a stingy woman. Mom and Grandma fought often. When they were at each other's throats, they were an equal match just like the two old chess players in the market. Neither one would back down. My earliest alleyway slang was all learned from them. But even I had a hard time uttering some of their swear words. I realized that women were more foul-mouthed than men. Grandma sometimes swore at me at the expense of my mother for no reason. I either ignored her or talked back. Once, I got serious.

"Keep her out of it."

"Who is she? Tell me, who is she?"

"You can snap at me, but not her."

"Wow, has she ever cooked for you, put you to bed, has she ever taken care of you? When did she ever act like a mom? As the saying goes, every child, even the one disfigured by a diseased scalp is handsome in the eyes of the mother. She treated you worse than the child with the diseased scalp!" Grandma pursed her lips in contempt.

"Keep her out of it, keep her out of it!" I started screaming at the top of my lungs.

Grandma stopped cursing Mom in my presence ever since.

"At the end of the day, mother is always the person you feel closest to. This little devil, no matter how well I treat him, the credit always goes to someone else. It's like I am buying crackers for others to enjoy," Grandma remarked to Huazi on her visit home one day. At the entrance of the alleyway, Huazi bought a bagful of freshly made candied chestnuts that were still piping hot. As I said before, Huazi liked me, she always brought something delicious for me on her home visit.

I am 13 years old now. Born in 1984, when both my parents

were working at a small factory in the alleyway. Grandma said that we were more like a family back then. Mom and Dad went to work during the day and were busy with the family after work. Life was like clockwork. With Grandma as his teacher, Dad learned to be a superb cook and was on the verge of surpassing the old master. When he cooked, the alluring aroma often wafted in and around the household from the kitchen. Dad had his special way in the kitchen. He always worked in a measured way and seemed relaxed, and he always managed to keep his clothes oil free no matter how busy, according to Grandma. Later as society opened up and workers were allowed to resign and strike out on their own, our family started to change until it fell apart. Dad no longer set foot in the kitchen for the fun of it.

I saw the pictures taken in those days. I was a fat boy with few hairs on my big head, very silly looking. Mom and Dad on the other hand were wearing fake and stiff-looking smiles. I don't like those pictures a bit. I still prefer the free wandering days and the Mom and Dad of those later years.

Dad resigned from his factory job and started a business as I learned to wander away from home. Mom also left the unit she had worked in and became the manager of a small restaurant. Dad later fell for a very young girl and put her up in a rental place on the sly. Then he would find all kinds of excuses to stay out all night. It wasn't too long after that Mom started coming home very late at night as well. Her story was that the restaurant was doing very well and the owner in a show of generosity had invited her to go karaoke, dancing, and have late night snacks with him. It was then that I got bored with playing chess.

Soon, Mom, Dad and I had reached a tacit understanding. They wouldn't force me to touch those stinky pieces again. In return, I wouldn't show any contempt for their behavior. I believed that such a resolution was a relief for all of us. Wanwan, also of the alleyway, was forced to practice piano daily under the supervision of her mother. She hated it so much that she wished she could cut out all her fingers. Wanwan was a willowy, very beautiful girl. She wanted desperately to go with me at night to the market place for play and fun around the counters, but she could only do that in her dreams. I was the lucky one compared to her.

Our household was in the Hongkou District of Shanghai. Our front door was facing the street and the back door was open to the alleyway so we called it the "back alleyway." The back alleyway was lined with the old-styled stone houses. They were old and dilapidated, and the stairs inevitably creaked with every footstep. We lived downstairs and Beibei's family lived upstairs. One of the floorboards leading upstairs had a hole in it. Every time I went to see Beibei, I always carelessly tripped at the spot. Once I even sprained my ankle because of it. In the back alleyway, there were faucets and water buckets in front of every household, some even added lean-tos by extending the eaves. According to Huazi, the alleyway was very clean during her childhood. There weren't this many people, and all these bicycles or mopeds. Not to mention the many buckets of all shapes. Both the upstairs and downstairs households shared the water faucets before, and things were rather simple. But now, the entrance was getting narrower and dirtier, blocked by useless fruit baskets and old crates people left there.

"We are seeing the consequences of population explosion." This was Huazi's studied observation. As someone who is a rainmaker at her unit, she was considered an experienced and knowledgeable person and known for her pithy remarks. She cited the next-door building where Shellac resided as an example. It was a building occupied by his parents and their five kids. When the kids became grown-ups and got married, they each took a room. Today, six families, including Shellac's parents, are living in this building, twenty-three people to be exact. Maybe it will have to accommodate a fourth generation as well. "This is an exponential increase." Huazi sounded compassionate and pessimistic.

People in our neighborhood are all waiting for relocation. Several consortia have been hankering after this piece of property. But after the household registration had been frozen for ten years, the demolition crew still has not descended upon our area. Grandma, recognized as a well-informed person, said that the problem had to do with a very important state agency that owned two western-styled buildings as well as a large, but older apartment building in the area. Rumor had it that their asking price was astronomical, in the hundred millions, and the consortia were having second thoughts about the deal. So all we could do was to wait patiently.

Many families in our alleyway are three-generation families. Some of the older generation ceded larger, south-facing rooms to the younger generation and retreated into the attic or the poorly-lit smaller rooms. Grandma who lived in the attic was a case in point, and so was Beibei's grandma who lived in a small and dark wing-room. They were all waiting anxiously for the day of relocation. Grandma said that after relocation, she would prefer to have a one-bedroom suite of her own instead of living a life of hell mixing with us. She never saw the day of relocation. She left us when I was 12.

I wasn't interested in being relocated. When Huazi got married, I lived at her place for two days and ran back home afterwards. The matchbox-like housing was too uniform and too neat for my taste. I found myself too boxed in, unable to move. The hallway was frighteningly quiet day and night. Nobody knew me and I didn't know anyone either. Huazi looked after me as if I were a prisoner. I wouldn't last for a day if I had to live a life like this.

My favorite TV shows were football and boxing matches. I loved playing wild games in the alleyways. How could I stay put inside?

There is one thing I never told Grandma. Huazi often had visitors who came with gifts. Her storeroom was well stocked with good wine, health supplements, and clothing along with all kinds of antiques, paintings, calligraphies, and chinaware. But I never saw Huazi sharing this good stuff. I hold a grudge against Huazi because of this. Dad seemed to be a generous soul in comparison, his stuff and Grandma's were always mixed together. Things were never separated into "yours" or "mine."

I have a special resemblance to Dad when he was young, according to Grandma.

"Your father was a trouble maker ever since he was a kid. During the Culture Revolution, he went to the tall building for fun and almost got killed by the various factions of activists." Grandma was more than happy to tell me about Dad's embarrassing past. The tall building was the nearby government office building. They said that during Cultural Revolution, you could hear the sound of crying, screaming, shouting, and beating coming from that building every night. Apparently, I was just as curious as Dad when he was a kid.

Dad said that he was only twelve at the time and he didn't know better. In those days, you could pretty much do anything if you were young, and become a hero or anti-hero overnight. He had been the victim of bullying and later he also bullied others. Even later, in order to ensure he was in top form, he went through harsh physical training, including weight lifting, boxing and throwing stone locks. It was what he and his friends did out of boredom. They became all brawn and no brains. He once dreamt of becoming a company leader because of the song he knew as a kid: "Company leader, company leader, when the cannon roars he is worth of ten thousand tales of gold." The rank of a company leader was once considered eminently high in the eyes of children who lived in the alleyway. Only when Dad tried to enlist at the age of 18, did he find out that the activists had branded him in a file as a hooligan at the age of twelve. His dream of becoming a company leader had been crushed for good. He learned through his own experience that this society was full of hypocrisy, fraud, violence, and evil.

What I have been through is no comparison to what he had been through, I missed those tumultuous years.

"Don't show your kindness too readily. Look at the beggars there, they may have a better life than we do. And the fellows with soft hands and in western suits may be able to strike killing blows in fighting. You need to watch out." When Dad and I walked on the street, he never missed the opportunity to teach me things. He is my best teacher in life.

In those days when Mom and Dad were mostly absent, I was a "wild" child, spending days and nights roaming around. The sound of Grandma calling for me could often be heard reverberating in the back alleyway.

At this time, Grandma's health was a far cry from her younger days. Her legs would ache for no reason, and sometimes she walked with a limp. When her feet hurt or when she was angry, she would curse and moan while lying in bed, or she would telephone Huazi or Jianguo to complain. Once, both Huazi and Jianguo were joining us for a New Year dinner, when the topic of Grandpa's condition came up. According to them, Grandpa spent his final days in the hospital in extreme pain and the doctor out of pity would give him a shot of Demerol at night. He bit his tongue, but he never complained. That had moved even the nurse to tears. Both Huazi and Dad were praising Grandpa for his courage at the table.

"Mom, if you were sick, you would surely give us a hard time. We would all be driven crazy and mad by you," Dad joked with Grandma.

"Right, right, Mom just loves to dramatize things. Who knows what would happen if her health fails. She would surely make all of us crazy first!" Huazi and Jianguo eagerly agreed.

"Hell, me? Dramatize? I am quite easy going. Look, I have trouble with my legs, but didn't I prepare the family dinner for you as usual? Human beings are not made of steel, what a pity. When the neighbors saw me limping around, they all felt sorry for me." Grandma showed her legs as she spoke.

"You see, you see, isn't this the beginning of her dramatization?" Dad and Huazi cried out laughing, and Grandma smiled in embarrassment.

That family dinner foreshadowed what was to come. Two years later, Grandma was diagnosed with diabetes and was hospitalized for the first time in her life. For the two weeks she was confined in the hospital, Dad and Huazi didn't even bother to pay her a visit. They both believed that it wasn't anything serious.

After her diagnosis, she started complaining endlessly, exactly as Dad had predicted. Either she would moan in pain and ask Huazi or Jianguo to immediately fetch her medication, or she would endlessly stress about the seriousness and peculiarity of her condition. She would carefully glean all the TV reports about diabetes and make a comprehensive analysis of her own condition. She knew at the time that hers was a difficult case and lamented that she wouldn't have long to live, "I am dying." Four years later, Grandma indeed left this world as a result of complications of diabetes. Grandma was an insightful person.

But Dad and Huazi didn't know diabetes that well. They simply assumed that Grandma was "dramatizing" her case. They also discovered that while Grandma was crying for medications she was hoarding a lot of painkillers and diabetes pills. They thought that she was acting up out of spite, a condition often seen among older people. At first, in a show of filial piety, they hired someone to help her out with the laundry on a part time basis, later they tried to be nice over the phone, but would never show up in person. Huazi, Dad and Jianguo jokingly talked about *The Boy Who Cried Wolf.* Huazi compared Grandma to the lying boy.

"Mom keeps saying that she is near death, or dying. One day when the wolf really comes, we will all become numb," Huazi said.

"Mom is overly dramatic. The other old lady of the back alleyway is also diabetic, but she still manages to buy groceries and cook. She even washes clothes, like any other healthy person." Jianguo nodded in agreement with Huazi.

"Mom has brought up five of us children. She was really hard-working when young. She did it all, sewing, mending, washing and starching. Now that she is old, she is a changed person, and a lazy one at that." Huazi was reminiscing about the old days.

"Hell, not living with her you have no idea how difficult she really is." Dad also joined the chorus of complaints.

"Sure, this is much ado about nothing and I am dramatizing my approaching death. Just watch out that one day you will regret it," Grandma responded when she overheard the exchanges between Huazi and Dad.

When Grandma passed away, doctors in the hospital concluded that she must have had the problem for quite some time. In recollection, Grandma must have been suffering from diabetes when she struggled up and down the alleyway, calling out my name for lunch or dinner.

This was unknown to Huazi and the others, or more precisely, they didn't have the patience to find out.

"Street Runner! Black Bug! It's meal time!" Grandma made her disheveled appearance in the alleyway in faltering steps. Her white hair tumbled about her face. Many people shook their heads and sighed.

"This family has no future. Only the old and the young are left behind, all others were gone. There is no hope."

"How many children does the old lady have?"

"I think five. Only Stinky Bug is with her now, and Stinky Bug is no good either. All the others don't even bother to show up anymore."

"What's the point of showing up? Haven't you seen that every time Meizi comes to visit, she is always the subject of her abuse? In her eyes, Meizi simply couldn't do nothing right. So upset, Meizi never set foot in this place again!" Meizi, whose name means plum in English, is my aunt who lives in Anhui.

"Oh, look, the Black Bug Street Runner is coming back! Street Runner, you should watch out for human traffickers!"

"Street Runner will never fall for them. He is daring and resourceful, they might fall for him instead." In a loud voice, Shellac laughingly interjected amidst the gathering crowd.

That was how I made my grand entrance into the alleyway, amid Grandma's call and neighbors' talk. Seeing that all eyes were on me, I felt that I really was someone to be reckoned with.

My best friends were Little Black Skin and One Bamboo. We were all over the alleyway, making sure that justice was done. For instance, we found the door one day to a household that was always closed, and a doorbell was installed outside. We were outraged. Doors to every household in the alleyway were always left open. We never tried to cover up or hide the way we lived. So we decided to retaliate. Taking turns, we all started ding dong ditching those people. We then observed the constant opening and closing of the door inside. They began to curse out of anger and desperation after a few nights. We were beside ourselves with happiness. They also tried to trap us pranksters. Fortunately, I learned from Dad at an early age how sinister the heart of a human being could be, and our actions became even more invisible, agile and frequent.

A week later, they finally had the doorbell uninstalled.

Little Black Skin, One Bamboo, and I had been to all the bridges that crossed the Suzhou River: the bridges at Sichuan Road, Henan Road, and Zhapu Road, and the Waibaidu Bridge, the list went on. The Postal Administrative Building at the foot of the Sichuan Road Bridge was our playground. We would slide down the banisters from high up, causing women to shriek with fright. When wandering around the Bund, we would talk to blond-haired blue-eyed foreign tourists with confidence. In Shanghainese we would say things like, "Hello, I will hit your head!" They would burst out laughing, having no idea what we just said. At the foot of the Waibaidu Bridge, I even got over the iron fence of the Russian Consulate, peed on the lawn and politely withdrew myself by the way I came in. I didn't make the mistake of intruding further onto the premises, since I knew that they were equipped with alarm systems and guards.

One summer, I even tried the waters of Suzhou River. While I was feeling my way along the riverbank, One Bamboo and Little Black Skin cried out from the shore because they got so scared. I soon jumped out after I found a dead rat floating in the water. It was a fact that I was not afraid of heaven or earth. The only thing that I truly dreaded were rats. The foul odor of the river also drove me away. I had to stay under the sun for quite a long time that day. I started on my way home once my underwear finally stopped sticking to my butt. Even today, I still regard Suzhou River as a filthy, but interesting river.

Wanwan's mother once sized me up and said "poor child." She was a school teacher. When I was old enough to carry a satchel on my back, I had a hard time sitting still. Staying in the classroom was pure agony. I hated teachers too. They either reported me or forced me to write characters as a punishment. Dad often offered goods from his store in exchange for passing grades. When I was forced to write characters, I often thought of Wanwan practicing piano. She not only had to write characters, she also needed to practice her piano. Wanwan was the real poor child. I reminisced about my carefree and enjoyable times at the Postal Administrative Building and the Russian Consulate.

The girl I liked the most in the back alleyway was Wanwan, although I hated her piano practicing. I told her that one day I would ask Dad and Mom to move to the attic so we could live together. Wanwan shook her head and said, "I don't want to stay in this lousy place in the future. I would like to live in a house with a garden and a beautiful swimming pool in the front. Then I would like to hire you as a part-time gardener." With a straight and stern face, I replied that I would kill her with scissors if I were to work there part-time. Wanwan burst out crying.

One time, I did run into a human trafficker. I was six at the time. It was probably winter. The hour was late, but I was still playing outside. A skinny woman pulled me over and touched me affectionately. I didn't like her and I didn't want her to touch me. The woman had a huge travel bag. "Little brother, do you know how to get to the railroad station?"

"Why don't you get a cab." My response was not exactly friendly.

"What is a cab?"

"A cab is a taxi. You are not from the city, are you?"

"Why are you so grouchy? I suppose you know the location of the railroad station. Are you able to show me the way?"

"Railroad station? I even know the way to the airport. Just follow me."

After leading the skinny woman for a short distance, I slipped away when we went past a hospital.

During the day, Beibei, One Bamboo and I would sometimes play at the hospital. One time, we peered through the glass to see the inside of the OB-GYN outpatient department. There was an exercise chart for pregnant women on the wall. One Bamboo and I tried the exercise movements and thought it was really fun. Beibei found our performance simply hilarious. She said that she would certainly come here to give birth to her child, a beautiful child. It was then that we unintentionally heard an exchange between two female doctors walking behind us.

"Tonight is going to be a big night. About ten women are going to give birth in the obstetrics department. Two of them may need cesarean section. The screams of the women in delivery are really annoying."

"You know what date is today? The date indicates 'prosperity.' They all say that children born today are incarnates of the God of Wealth. Didn't you notice that the woman in bed eight insisted on having Doctor Zhu give her the C-section today! I have no idea what medicine these would-be-mothers took so they could give birth today!"

"They put their lives at risk. Gee, what a crowd here. With ten more births, Shanghai's housing market will be further squeezed." The female doctors chuckled as they moved beyond earshot.

As I went past the hospital with the skinny woman, I noticed that the lawn in the courtyard seemed quiet and the lights in some of the rooms were still on. I could sense the atmosphere of waiting, waiting for the arrival of the babies. The hospital at this time seemed much more of an interesting playing ground than the shabby train station, so I ducked into a hiding place inside the hospital fence. The skinny woman was crying out for me in a suppressed voice.

"Little brother! Little brother! Where are you hiding? Come out now, let's take the cab together!"

As I said before, I didn't like skinny women. I wouldn't be tempted even if she offered to fly with me on an airplane. I slipped into the hospital building without looking back.

I didn't find anything interesting inside the hospital that night. Outside the tightly closed maternity ward, I saw a dozen or so men who all looked worn-out and stressed. I could also hear terrifying howls and piercing screams. As I managed to slip into the ward, the scene of a woman with her legs wide open came into view. There were people holding her shoulders down with all their might, and a doctor in white robe was almost completely on her, using his knees pushing against her big belly. The woman was yelling, crying, and struggling in excruciating pain when all of a sudden blood rushed out from her lower body. I immediately fled the scene feeling horrified. I thought someone had been killed.

Afterwards, I heard the baby's cry. I didn't expect childbirth to be so terrifying and bloody. I was so dazed that I only found the gate after circling the premises several times. In a mad dash, I asked the deserted city streets at this wee hour, "Did I also arrive in this world at such a dark moment and amid the screams of my mom?" I was soon home and I told Grandma of my encounter with the skinny woman, but I didn't dare to venture into my experience at the hospital. Grandma said, "As giblets are difficult to clean, it is just as difficult to know what's on somebody's mind. This skinny woman though, she must have been a trafficker."

"Do you know that they will take you to the countryside, force you to work your head off during the day, then take off your clothes and tie you up at night? You would be fed with husks and covered with straw. Otherwise, they would cut your Achilles' tendon or cut off your hand, break your legs or arms, and force you to beg in town or collect garbage for a living ..." Grandma was still mumbling when I lied down in bed.

I started screaming at the top of my lungs, out of fear, but also in protest. Grandma covered her ears and cut short her horrifying stories. The piercing screams lasted for a long, long time. Whenever I decided to throw a tantrum, my screams would awaken the whole alleyway. Many windows opened up in an instant.

"Was there a fire? An earthquake? What happened?"

"What earthquake? Nonsense! As I have guessed, it is Street Runner again!"

"Like father, like son. Stinky Bug was a rascal while young. Black Bug Street Runner, this little rascal will grow up a gangster as well! Capable of committing murder and arson!"

"There is no hope for this unruly child! Have you seen how he torments his Grandma during the day? What a pity!"

"What can you do? His parents are aloof. Who are you to weigh in? Like they say, the emperor is not worried, why should the eunuchs?"

In those days, Grandma and I were basically the only two members of our family. Dad rarely came home. He treated the situation like a fait accompli to force Mom to agree to a divorce. Mom slept during the day and went out at night, always by herself. She was obviously too busy to care for me. And Grandma was the only one left. She had no choice, but to take care of me. I didn't understand why Mom always worked the night shift, wearing heavy makeup and even dying her hair blond. It was as if she was going to a grand ball held at some foreign embassy. Grandma had own her malicious explanation for mom's get up, which I absolutely would not repeat in here. I don't care for Mom, but I didn't want to hear Grandma disparaging her either. I felt that Grandma was estranged from Mom. Their importance to me might be different, but nonetheless real.

Mom once talked about going to Japan out of the blue. She

tried to borrow money for the trip, phoning Huazi, Jianguo for help, and even called long distance to Beijing where an uncle of mine had relocated. According to Grandma, he was a very important official in a very important state governmental department. I have never met this uncle. He showed up at Grandpa's funeral, hurried back soon after, and never set foot in his old house in Shanghai again. Even today, some people still talk about the black car parked for two days at the alleyway entrance for his own personal use. Rumor had it that he had been in Shanghai several times on official business, but he selflessly chose not to pay a visit to Grandma on the side. Grandma never confirmed or denied the veracity of the story. She said, "Even the emperor has poor relatives and it may be a good thing that he stays away. The day he shows up, must be the day I report to the Lord of Death."

Uncle didn't respond to Mom's plea for financial help, he just called Grandma. Grandma said she knew what woman like Mom would do in Japan. "Nowadays, we can be ashamed of poverty, but we need to maintain our morals. She is going to Japan to sell her body and flesh!" Upon hearing that, Uncle never returned Mom's call.

After learning that Mom went to Uncle for help, Dad was so infuriated that he gave Mom a good beating. Mom rolled up into a ball in bed and cried bitterly.

"You should never seek help from my elder brother, even if it means that you have no one to turn to but the king of heaven! You are a disgrace," Dad said.

As the story goes, it was Uncle who bailed Dad out after he suffered a severe beating at the hands of the Red Guard activists at a young age. Uncle is ten years senior than Dad and was already swaggering in police uniforms at the time.

"Look at you, what else are you, but a hooligan? What a disappointment! Everyone in my work unit now knows that I have a hooligan brother who has been detained at the activist headquarters. You have brought shame to your brother. How do you expect me to serve the revolution in the future? If it weren't for the pleading tears of Mom, I would never allow you to drag my good name through the mud!" Uncle grumbled in anger and walked in front with big strides.

"To hell with you! You're the scandal! You looked so abject and apologetic in front of those people. You are a coward! Damn it, I didn't ask for your help! I am going back in, I would rather be beaten to death!" Dad huffed and turned, running towards the tall building. In an instant, Uncle blocked his way and held his arm in a lock.

"From now on, don't you ever ask me for help, Stinky Bug!" Driven by anger, Uncle gave Dad a sound beating with no further explanation, and managed to drag him home.

They became sworn enemies from then on and stopped communicating with each other. Not long afterwards, Uncle got promoted and moved to Beijing, and they were never back on good terms again.

Mom's attempts to borrow money from Huazi and Jianguo also went nowhere. In the end, she never went to Japan. But the strange thing was that Dad decided to give Mom a gift of five thousand yuan (1 yuan equals to 0.16 US dollars). I later found out by accident that Dad meant to buy her out, so that she would leave us, the farther the better. After learning the truth, I felt for Mom, although we had not been close for quite some time.

She is my Mom after all. I still remembered that one time, on an impulse, she cooked a leg of pork for me that I enjoyed for three whole days. I bragged about it in front of Beibei each of those three days.

"My Mom bought it for me. It was huge and weighed so much …"

"I don't like it, it's mostly fat, so disgusting," she said.

"Hell, your mother never bought it for you, she doesn't care for you!" I said right back at her.

"It's your mother who dislikes you! You only know the triangular market, have you been to Jinjiang Amusement Park?"

"What is Jinjiang Amusement Park, it is not cool anymore!

Have you ever tried the sauna or got a massage? Over there, a woman in bikini held me close to clean my ears, the lounge is air-conditioned, and serves cold drinks, You can also watch VCD ... Huh, you haven't, have you? Nothing but a country bumpkin," I said.

"You are a hoodlum! A Garbage wretch ..." Beibei muttered at me.

"You are a slug! You are ugly. The woman in the bathhouse is much more beautiful than you."

I made a wry grimace at Beibei. She cried and went upstairs. I felt triumphant. So far, I was the only one who had been to a sauna among my friends. It was all thanks to Dad. As for the bikini part of the story, that was made up. But such scenes are often seen on TV, and they were definitely not my fabrication.

The day Dad took me for a bath, he hailed a taxi to a five-star hotel, and we had our sauna there. In fact, the steam room experience was more like a living hell for me. Plus, I didn't like to sit naked right next to other people. Looking at my penis and thinking about my nickname Black Bug, I felt rather ashamed of myself. Since I refused to sit still, Dad got mad and shooed me out of the room.

After fleeing the steam room, I had a great time in the luxurious lounge by gulping down more than my share of beverages. I had polished off ten cans of cola by the time Dad emerged from the steam room red-faced. Dad paid an enormous price for those drinks. Fortunately, he was rich and paid the bill in style, without asking any questions. According to the neighbors, Dad has always been a bottomless coffer, a spendthrift in Shanghai dialect, ever since he was a child. When Dad took me out and hailed for a taxi, I would stay very close to him. Sensing that we were being watched, I deliberately prolonged the motion of getting into the cab. I hoped that more people would see my happiness and how Dad loved and cherished me.

Once, Little Black skin, One Bamboo and I took a taxi together and went to Wujiao Square looking for our dads who were there playing mahjong for money. I remember it was late at night on New Year's Day. After we got in the cab, the driver lamented that the times had really changed. Children at the ages of six or seven could hail a taxi.

Sitting next to the driver, I told him that growing up that I never rode the bus and always took the taxi. I didn't lie at all. After I was born, Huazi borrowed a luxury Lincoln from her friends and took me home. I was told that the car was quite a standout those days on the Shanghai Bund. Huazi is a very resourceful person. Unfortunately, I not only vomited and peed on the Lincoln, I also wouldn't stop screaming. That really upset Huazi. We switched to a cab halfway through, and the strange thing is that I broke into a smile the minute we got into a shabby Xiali, the brand name of a cheap Chinese car. Huazi joked that I was doomed to grow up poor. Every time I went out with Dad after this, we always chose a Xiali taxi.

"It's my good fortune that the car I am driving is Xiali, or I would have missed the opportunity of knowing you young gentlemen." From his accent, it seems that the driver with a crooked nose was from the northern part of Jiangsu Province.

"You are right. When I have a car of my own one day, I will drive myself around." While chitchatting with him, I also gave him directions. I had been there before with Dad—his friend's house at Wujiao Square—and I knew the way.

"Wow, you certainly sound older than your age. The kids today are so incredible. They seem to know so much. Our society has really opened up." Crooked Nose chuckled, as if he was surprised by my remarks.

"What's so special about buying a car? If you are really rich, go buy a mansion in Hongqiao. Don't you want to marry Wanwan? Wanwan wants a house, not a car." One Bamboo tapped my shoulder from behind and mocked me with that snide remark.

"I don't want to marry Wanwan! Hell, you go and marry

her!" With my face as red as a beet, I slapped his hand hard on my shoulder.

"Why are you getting all worked up? Your face is red. If you don't want her, why do you follow her around all day long? Your dick must be itchy and you want to fuck her. Do you think I don't know that?" One Bamboo shoved my shoulder with force. He went too far this time.

"You are the one who is horny, you swine! You are One Bamboo, a bamboo is a penis, you smelly penis!" Unable to suppress my anger, I turned to grab One Bamboo's collar in one quick swoop to slap him. He was not someone easy to deal with either. He held my shoulder and rammed me with his head.

"Is it real that someone is named One Bamboo? It is a fitting name for a boy though. C'mon, be more civilized with your tongue, young gentlemen ... Stop fighting, or I will take you to the police!" Crooked Nose warned us, at once angry and amused.

"We are minors, you don't need to scare us." Little Black Skin calmly retorted as One Bamboo and I returned to our seats.

"I give up, I give up. With kids like you, Shanghai will have a future. Why, you are all so outstanding. We are catching up with the world."

Wasn't that obvious? We three proudly looked at each other and unexpectedly broke out laughing. We were so happy, our laughter, like the shattered glass broken by Dad in a rage, came falling down on the quiet pavement.

As we arrived at Wujiao Square, we each paid five yuan and bade goodbye to Crooked Nose. I meant to brag about my good luck with girls, but the ride was too short. I once met a girl on the street who made a pass at me and that has caused a lot of envy on the part of One Bamboo and Little Black Skin.

That night, in one of the buildings at Wujiao Square we found Dad. Every one of them was stunned when the door was knocked open. They couldn't believe their eyes. Our alleyway was at least ten bus stops away from Wujiao Square, and all buses had long stopped running at this hour.

"Such a long distance, how did you get here?" Shellac was looking at his son, Little Black Skin. Little Black Skin looked at One Bamboo, and One Bamboo looked at me.

"It must be the wretch, the Street Runner's sordid idea. You took a cab, right?" Dad came out and forcefully held me into his arms.

I nodded. Buried inside my Dad's hug, I greeted all of them with a sincere smile. Dad is the one I most admire in this world. He understood the need to enjoy life unlike those idiots who had lots of money, but chose to pinch and save. Dad said that there are always people in this world who couldn't let go of things. I am just like Dad. When I had money, I got excited thinking about how I would spend it. When I didn't have money, I would get gloomy and often pick fights with Grandma.

From Dad, I learned to fight, use abusive language, hail a cab, and enjoy the sauna. My best toy was a ragged bike. I moved in it like a flying bird in the alleyway. I am grateful to Dad for never pressuring me to do anything. That's how I became an independent and free spirit and was at ease among adults. I owe all my understanding of the city to Dad's hands free attitude towards me.

That night, Dad and the others settled us in another room where we had a great time. We had late night snacks, played arcade games, watched Hong Kong martial art films on video. One Bamboo, Little Black Skin and I also had a raucous fistfight on the carpet. We didn't even know when we fell sleep sprawled out there on the carpet. When we woke up the next day at noon, Dad and the others were still playing mahjong. The noise of tiles clattering against each other was a testament to that. Seeing milk, bread, and stuffed steam buns on the table, I sensed that it was a day filled with a festive atmosphere.

In those days when my Dad was absent, I was particularly nasty with Grandma, tormenting her to no end. I didn't know why I acted that way. Every time Grandma had meals ready, I simply ignored them. But when she took the bowl and chopsticks away, I would cry out that I was hungry. I deliberately dropped rice grains all over the place. Wearing dirty shoes, I jumped hard on Grandma's bed, leaving prints all over her bed linens. Grandma was a heavy smoker and a tea drinker. I would throw her most precious tea can in the alleyway, sink her cigarettes in water, and hide her cigarette lighter under the bed. I had also been thinking of throwing her mahjong set to the top of the tall building. Grandma was no match for me.

"I beg you, little devil, please stop! My young gentleman!"

I was not moved.

"Stinky seven and stroppy eight. You are such a nuisance! No one is going to clean the sheets for me. You are killing me! What have I done to deserve this …"

"I want ice cream, I want Wangwang's rice cake!" I saw the opportunity for blackmail and could usually get what I want.

Once in a while, I worked in cahoots with Grandma, too. For instance, Mom usually hogged the bathroom early in the morning and deliberately dragged her feet in there when Grandma needed to go badly. I would fiercely pound on the bathroom door. Assuming that I needed to go, Mom would reluctantly cede her "treasure island" to me. But the minute Mom came out, Grandma would immediately slip her way in. As for me, I would be long gone by then. For that, both Mom and Grandma would call me an "idiot" many times.

When Grandma got really upset, she would try to strike me. I would escape towards the back alleyway on purpose and play the chicken game with Grandma, dodging and evading her every move. Scenes of me being chased by Grandma were all too familiar in the alleyway. Grandma stopped chasing once she realized that I was provoking her intentionally. Instead, she would scold me loudly in the alleyway.

The one card Grandma had up her sleeve was sending Dad a beeper message for help. "Be home soon for important family business." When Dad rushed home, she would embellish her story, describing me as an unmitigated evil. Naturally, I would then get a good beating from Dad.

A few times, I was beaten black and blue and couldn't get up at all. Grandma would whimper at my bedside and grumble that Dad went overboard and the beating was too vicious.

"Why blame the child? Have you set a good example yourself? Everything is upside down nowadays. Fathers don't act like fathers, mothers don't act like mothers, and no one is afraid of being talked about by others!"

"I've had it. I know you are criticizing me by insinuation. When I was young, the old man used to beat the crap out of me, too. What is this in comparison?" Dad said.

"Did I say anything wrong? You rarely show up here, and this is the way you act the minute you are here?" Grandma snapped back.

"But you are the one who beeped me. I wash my hands from whatever happens from now on."

"Your son needs to be fed. You cannot leave all that to me. I am old, and no longer have the energy to take care of him."

"Why don't you let him eat outside, what's wrong with a box lunch? What did we have to eat when we were small? All those people sitting around the table had to share one dish and one soup, without even a drop of oil in sight. Haven't we all grown up alright?"

"So you were all blown up and fed by wind alone? Didn't you have more than your share of pork butt, chickens and ducks? Have you forgotten you used to swoop in and stuff yourself without any concern for others, including your parents?" Grandma's face was all red as a result of the agitation, but Dad had already left in a huff by that time.

On the side of our building facing the street, there were several small vendors selling lousy box lunches at noontime. Most of their customers were migrant workers, small shop owners from outside the city, cab drivers, and a small number of nearby residents.

I don't like box lunches. There was a time when Grandma was too sick to do grocery shopping and I had to settle for box lunches for days in a row. I got nauseated the very second I set my eyes on a box lunch. Dad and Grandma were first-rate chefs, but both gave up on cooking. Although, Dad didn't have an excuse like Grandma.

When Dad was doing well financially, he took me to eat in restaurants, too. Dad was a generous soul, his philosophy is: no money left over, no butt sore. He would often order many dishes for his guests, including men and women, and his friends and foes. I guessed the femme fatale must be one of the invitees. I couldn't understand why Dad would invite his foes. Dad's response was that "at times you need to be patient, and smile at your foes." Dad often talked about profound life lessons that he thought that I would put to good use one day.

Once, Grandma cryptically asked me to pay attention to the women in Dad's life, but I was too busy eating to notice them. Plus, I couldn't really tell them apart. They all seemed white as jade under the light, as if they were immortals. I can't even piece together an image of the kind-hearted young woman who often sat right next to me. I do remember that she paid even closer attention to my dishes than me. I only cared about the sumptuous dishes on the table.

In spite of Grandma's complaint about Dad's vicious beating of me, she would still call for Dad's help when I had exhausted her patience. Sometimes she would use that as a threat, but being a heartless creature who never gave up until the very end, I almost literally courted for Dad's furious beatings.

At six, I went to the Phoenix Mountain Public Cemetery for the first time to visit Grandpa's grave. I never knew Grandpa since I was born about the same time he died. As Dad pointed out, it was also the year that Shanghai was hit by earthquakes. Many people were so panicked that they jumped from their high rise buildings to escape and got seriously wounded, some even died, but those who stayed inside their homes with resignation emerged from the quakes unscathed. The fact that Grandpa and I did this life and death relay at this unusual time made me believe that there was some kind of mysterious link between us. Standing in front of the small grave, I couldn't understand how Grandpa could lie underneath there. I learned from Dad that Grandpa was an exceptionally stern person who had never smiled at Dad and never allowed Dad to climb on his shoulders to pee. But Dad always sounded full of respect when he spoke of him. He said that Grandpa came to Shanghai sixty years ago with nothing in his pocket and managed to feed and clothe all members of his family, which was no small accomplishment. But his most impressive feat was that he had this aura about him wherever he sat. No children nearby dared to utter a peep.

"When I was small, I had to hold my breath every time I walked past him." Dad lamented time and again in front of Grandpa's grave.

Whoever could make Dad hold his breath must be someone extraordinary. Everybody was in awe when speaking of Grandpa. Jianguo often showed me the scar on his head, the result of "the old man's" beating, according to him. At the old man's bidding, they were asked to "walk like a wind, stand like a pine, sit like a bell and sleep like a bow." Since Jianguo didn't stand up straight, he was slapped by Grandpa and was sent hurtling to the other end of the alleyway.

"I wonder how he managed to exert so much strength with a slap?" Jianguo reminisced the event without any bitterness. Maybe, death can serve as a distiller and after distillation, life becomes pure, great and is given a shroud of mystery.

Grandma always talked about how Grandpa held on to his life because he wanted to see me come into this world.

"You were not a good baby. You refused to grant him this satisfaction before he left. When visiting his grave, you have to kneel down and kowtow three times in earnest and promise him to be an exemplary son and grandson, or Grandpa would never forgive you." Grandma instructed me repeatedly before my trip to Suzhou.

"Father, your grandson Gu Longfei is here to see you. The neighbors all say that Gu Longfei looks just like you. Please bless him, your grandson …" Huazi spoke seriously to the tombstone. Aside from my kindergarten teacher, I rarely heard people call me by my proper name. I stood there rigid and holding my breath, much like Dad and Jianguo when they were young in spite of my feeling that Huazi sounded ridiculous. That was an indelible solemn moment in my memory.

"Father, I am now learning to be a businessman like you. Please bless me with good fortune from down there. According to Mother, you had been a scalper and a broker while young, and had run a cigarette stand as well. In a way, you were a small business owner. Be sure to bless me …" mumbled Dad in a low voice in front of the tomb. He then burned the incense and lighted the candles, seemingly very devout.

Jianguo said nothing, just bowed again and again. I noticed that he was standing ramrod straight.

I could sense the majestic power of Grandpa while alive.

I had this image of Grandpa as a handsome, stern, mysterious and towering knight figure. I believe that Grandpa must have had a femme fatale as his company. Otherwise, why would he chose to stay in Suzhou all by himself and among the white tombstones of this strange-looking Phoenix Mountain? At Dad's direction, I also carefully and piously burned the incense and kowtowed to Grandpa. This was the first time ever that I behaved myself so properly and so well.

At the graveyard, I learned to respect death and appreciate that death is a more mysterious existence than life. Grandma also "left us" all of a sudden when I was twelve, Dad and I held her ash in our hands and buried her alongside Grandpa. In sobs, Dad asked the cremation urn, "Mom, I kept you worried for forty years. Next time when I am in trouble, who is to admonish me?" I was in the same situation as Dad. Without Grandma, I would have no one to fight with, no one to throw temper tantrums at in retaliation. And who was going to fondly call me an "idiot"? When these thoughts went through my mind, tears came to my eyes.

There were also times when I was an obedient kid to Grandma. I always complied when she asked me to call Huazi or Jianguo since she couldn't remember their phone numbers, and I always behaved myself when she gave me pocket money. Both Huazi and Jianguo liked me very much and they brought me gifts and snacks every time they came. However, their feelings for me had their limits, too. Take Jianguo for instance, his gift to me never exceeded ten yuan, but all his gifts to my cousin Xiaoli were worth at least a hundred yuan each. That reminded me of a conversation from this one TV program. A man says that he would spend a hundred yuan for a gift to the child of his lover, and ten yuan for his own child. I figured that cousin Xiaoli must be the child of Jianguo's lover.

There was a high school on Nanxun Road not far from our place. Grandma told me that Uncle went to this high school a long time ago when it was "St. Francis High School," a Catholic school with over a hundred years history. There was a huge clock on the school tower, visible from hundreds of meters away. I liked the huge clock very much. Its chimes had reverberated in my head as long as I can remember, and have probably been incorporated into my pulse. The clock was probably over a hundred years old, according to Grandma. It was a gift to "St. Francis" from a high official of the Qing Dynasty (1644–1911). Grandma so trusted this clock that she always asked me to check its time before sending me to school, getting someone ready for the train station, and watching her most favorite TV series. I was more than happy to comply. With the passage of time, it became a routine for Grandma to ask me, "Black Bug, what time is it now?" The big clock symbolized a shared understanding and joy between Grandma and me.

The fondest name Grandma gave me was "idiot." Grandma would call me this every time I proudly bragged about what I ate on one of my restaurant trips with Dad, scampered up and down Huazi's body and refused to let go of her when she dropped in to see Grandma, and when I rushed to say hello to the beautiful Wanwan as she walked passed our door. And I would retort without hesitation by calling her an "idiot" as well. This was considered the best moment of our cordial relationship.

During her last hospitalization, I took Aunt Meizi to see her. She had just regained consciousness and in a low voice she mumbled "idiot" the minute she saw me. I immediately returned the favor by calling her the same. Hearing this, Meizi and Auntie Wu, the hired nursing assistant, were taken aback. But eventually they burst out laughing. Even the usually grim-faced Grandma who was so ravaged by illness cracked a rare smile. Meizi mused that Grandma smiled because her grandson came to visit. I lowered my head and said nothing. It was at a moment like this that I realized and understood what the lyrics of the song "silence is golden" meant.

I came to know a long time ago that I actually never hated Grandma. My teasing her and giving her a hard time was only my way of existence. Ignored mostly by the world, I only had Grandma's shoulder to lean on. For more than a decade, Grandma and I shared a life under the same roof. She had abused me verbally, but never physically. She never lavished me with expensive delicacies or toys, but she struggled to boil water and cook for me. Her care for me was simple and solid. The colorful adages that came out of her mouth effortlessly were idiomatic, but not vulgar, and far more instructive than textbooks. Her words and deeds reflected the hundreds of years of Shanghai alleyway culture. Huazi and Jianguo paid for her daily expenses. Grandma once commented that it had been thirty years since she had new clothes made for herself. Yet at every Chinese New Year, the lucky money she gave me was more than what I got from Huazi, Jianguo, and Dad. At other times, I was never shy from milking money from her by hook or by crook. The pleasure I had whenever I succeeded in getting her largesse led me to believe that Grandma's love for me came only next to Dad's. I measured people's love for me in terms of money.

Many of the households in the alleyway had a tiny plaque on their doors: A Five-Virtues Family. Not ours. Our family was a boisterous one. We always fought, Grandma, Dad, Mom, and me. Sometimes Huazi and Jianguo were also involved in our fights during their visits. Every time Aunt Meizi from Anhui Province came, she was sure to pick up a fight with someone as well. Ours should have named more aptly as a "five-quarrels family."

Beibei said she often heard us squabbling downstairs, but couldn't tell who was fighting with whom. Beibei tried to figure out what was going on by listening through the walls and she would then pass the story on to her grandma. Like Grandma, her grandma simply loved to pass rumors around.

Dad liked to throw things around when he got angry. Usually, he would reach for objects on the table, and bowls and dishes would fly in all directions when he loss control. Mom called it his crazy moment. Once he freaked out at an exchange between Grandma and Mom, and threw a stool at the window, shattering the glass. Mom sneered at him and said, "If you are a man, why don't you smash the TV and the microwave? The only two things of value in the household!"

Once big events like this happened, Grandma would always call Huazi afterwards to complain that she would lose it in a rage if she stayed one more day. But she would refuse Huazi's offer to take her in, saying that in the event of death, she would rather die at her own home.

"Your brother Stinky Bug forced me to sign a piece of paper that promises to leave half of this house to that woman! He is the last of our line. Indeed the last one! All he wants is to have her agree to a divorce." Grandma always referred Mom disparagingly as "that woman."

"My brother? What do you mean? Isn't he your son? So did you sign it?"

"No, I didn't. I may be doddering, but my mind is clear. If I signed, would I still have a place to live in the future? The last of our bloodline threw away my teacup and broke the Walkman you gave me. He asked me to move in with you. You should have seen the way he looked, it was really scary! He wanted to force my hand and chase me away ..."

"Why don't you stay with me for a few days until the storm passes? If you are not around, no one can sign the paper. I can drop in to find about the details. This is not a simple matter. My name is still in the household registry and I have a say on the matter since I also have a share," said Huazi.

"You can run, but you can't run forever. I am not coming. For the time being, you should stay away. The scoundrel is not acknowledging any relatives or friends these days. I heard him swear to himself that he would make no concessions to anyone. Yesterday, Auntie Li of the Residential Committee came to mediate and he chased her away the minute she set foot inside the apartment. Auntie Li was the one who helped him return to Shanghai from the cooperative in the countryside. She was really pissed off that he wouldn't even show her respect in return. I was thinking of convincing him to open up a restaurant here since I know he wasn't doing well with the store."

"You are still trying to help him out! It was your doting that made Stinky Bug what he is today. He was quite a handful when he was small. None of the other siblings are quite like him!"

"So it is my fault again. What did I do wrong? You children are like my fingers. I cherish you all. Did I ever shortchange you when you were young? Have I ever asked you to do household chores with your dainty hands? You can also check with Meizi if she ever suffered during her days in the countryside. Her living expenses were sent monthly from Shanghai. Once she had the money, she pretended to be too sick to work the fields. She wasn't there to do physical labor, she was there as a tourist …"

Huazi interrupted in frustration. "Ok, ok, you won. We were all apples of your eye and we all had a wonderful bourgeois life, eating well and living comfortably. Ok? Alas, Stinky Bug is really stinky! The apartment is ours. His wife is someone who married into our family, and she has no right to the apartment. But without arriving at a settlement on the house, the court is not going to rule on the divorce. They just have to wait, probably forever. Where is he now?"

"He never returned after yesterday's fight. I figure he went over there. The bitch told me early this morning that with or without my signature, she was determined to have this apartment. Someone she knew at the court is going to make that happen. Huazi, do you know someone at the court?" Grandma asked.

"There" was a reference to the other household Dad maintained. I received many phone calls from a woman looking for Dad. I knew immediately that the caller was the femme fatale, so I told Grandma that the calls were from "there." Grandma would say to me, "Stop saying that. What do you know about 'there' anyway?"

"Mom, don't you listen to her. This is Shanghai, a big city, not a small town where anything is possible. Even knowing the mayor of Shanghai is not going to make any difference. Your name is on the deed, and no one dares to rule the case without your consent."

"You'd better make sure. That woman knows how make things go her way. Once the ruling is made, it will be too late. After living here for fifty years, I never expected that one day I would be forced to live on the street. I am eighty years old now and can only move about with difficulty. What have I done to deserve this? May heaven have pity on me, a poor woman at the end of her life. Oh, I must have sinned in my previous life …"

Grandma whimpered into the phone.

"Mom, rest assured, there is no way that that could happen! Housing in divorce cases is of critical importance. The court would never take it lightly. Even if a ruling is really issued, I can hire a lawyer to appeal the case on your behalf. Don't cry! Just wait there and wait for them to ask your opinion."

"I am begging you now. If you don't do anything, you will certainly regret it when I die! Old man, why did you leave me so early? I have no one to depend on now!" Grandma sniffled in tears.

"Alright, I will ask someone for help. Mommy, will you please control yourself? I have a friend who runs a law firm. I will ask him to act on your behalf when the time comes." Huazi sometimes addressed Grandma as Mom and sometimes as Mommy. I found out "Mommy" was usually reserved for more serious situations.

"I must tell you also that I've had enough of the Black Bug Street Runner. He gives me a hard time every day."

"I am not getting myself involved with you and Black Bug. He is your pride and joy. You don't suppose I know that, do you? If he stays quiet, you would provoke him into a fight. I have witnessed that several times," said Huazi.

"So, I was the one who asked for trouble. Is there a place where I can have real justice? All my explanations fall on deaf ears! By the way, buy me a pair of plastic slippers from the department store next time you come. It is getting hot and I will be needing them."

"Mom, I can't do everything for you. I don't have time to shop. Ask Stinky Bug or Street Runner to buy them for you."

"Stinky Bug is more like a will-o'-the-wisp, a flash that disappears before you can catch it. He is so disrespectful. He is trying to be a lord over me. How can I ask him to do anything for me? If you can't, I'll just make do without them."

"I can't spare the time to buy them, but I can bring you a new pair of slippers of mine. Mom, I dropped by to see Meizi when I went to Hefei for a meeting."

Huazi switched the subject to Meizi on the phone.

"Please don't talk about her. She is no longer a daughter of mine. For eight years, I haven't received even one letter from her. As the saying goes, even if you cut off all your connections, always leave your line of communication open with your mother. Does she regard me as her mother at all?" Grandma was in a huff. I heard that Meizi left Shanghai for a village in Anhui Province at the age of sixteen to work the fields and became a worker four years later at a factory in Hefei. During a winter time family visit eight years ago, she had a falling-out with Grandma and left angrily that night in snow. And we never heard from her ever since.

"Mom, Meizi told me that she missed you often. So much that she sometimes cried." Huazi obviously was trying to cover up for Meizi. I found out that Huazi was friendly with Meizi, but she kept her distance from Dad so that she didn't have to confront him.

"She is an idiot who followed her emotions and not her head. Eight years ago, she came with her daughter and was displeased at the way I spoke Mandarin to her child. She complained that I deliberately spoke with an accent particular to the people who lived north of the Yangtze River, a sure sign that I looked down upon them. She claimed that she was not from north of the Yangtze River ... But I didn't do it on purpose, I just couldn't pronounce the words in Mandarin properly. She's an idiot! Her daughter left without even calling me 'Grandma.' Grandchildren from your daughter's side are just like dogs. They leave after they finished eating," Grandma grumbled to Huazi.

"Mom, these things are so trivial. Just let it go. Meizi is not a bad person, just a little simple-minded. Remember how she was severely beaten by those hooligans in the countryside? Maybe she suffered some brain damage as well. She also had a strong ego. What she hated the most was to be treated like a non-native Shanghainese. Her daughter Zhimin, as a child of the educated youth sent to the countryside, is qualified to gain residency in Shanghai. Did you know that?"

"I get it now. Meizi must have asked you for help, right? So she finally remembered me when she realized that I might help her daughter regain residential status in Shanghai. That's what she had in mind. Even if you want to catch a chicken, you need a handful of rice. Nothing is going to fall from the sky! Huazi, you stay away from this matter. You are polite and friendly with everyone and know how to put in a good word for others. But I am not going to agree to that!" Grandma warned Huazi in no uncertain terms and hung up.

This was the first time I saw Grandma lose her temper with Huazi. She even talked about her interpersonal skills with sarcasm.

Huazi is indeed a very capable person in our family. She is the head of the advertising department of a huge enterprise. She's in charge of tens of millions of advertising money. Usually, she was surrounded by at least a hundred men seeking favors from her. Therefore, many people considered her a very powerful person and wanted a presence in her circle. She did us some small favors with her position as well, such as car services at no charge, electronic products at factory prices, and passing on holiday gifts from the enterprise at no cost to her. She also often supplied cigarettes for Grandma. Like Jianguo, the smart Huazi remembered the relatives of her own family, Grandma and me, in her measured ways.

But she hoarded the Napoleon XOs, Brand's chicken essence, fur coats, cashmere sweaters, beautiful china, scrolls of calligraphy, and paintings at her place. Those things never made their way to our home. Apparently, she didn't think expensive stuff went well with the alleyway milieu of the common people.

And now Huazi tried to put in a good word for Meizi and Zhimin. Running from office to office, Grandma got so exhausted with Zhimin's residency permit that her legs almost gave up on her. She did it all because Huazi mentioned it in passing. Meizi never uttered a word of thanks to Grandma. She instead regarded Huazi as her gracious benefactor.

It took Grandma's wisdom to see through Huazi as "always

the polite and friendly one."

After his last fight with Grandma, Dad didn't come home for a long time. Those were the darkest days of my life. Stewing with anger, Grandma just lied in bed sulking. Her thoughts were only with Dad. And I had to settle for box lunches meal after meal. It was the time right after the winter equinox, a time with frequent cold snaps. This usually made the box lunches cold and tasteless. Everyone knew that Grandma doted on Dad the most. He was the youngest among all the children. Legend has it that the youngest one is always a free spirit with the most subversive character, and a driving force for social development. But according to our neighbors, Dad was the most "incongruous" one among all of the children. He was the most handsome one, but also the only one who never made it, a judgment that I beg to differ. I could sense the unusual wonderful quality that distinguished Dad from all others. Running against traditional norms, he was the most extraordinary among the ordinary. And I have inherited those outstanding qualities from him.

They say that Grandma was fast asleep when he was born. She was actually surprised to find a bundle of joy next to her when she woke up, thinking that it was all a dream. Grandma said that all of the other four children's births had been life-and-death experiences for her except Dad's, hence, her special feelings for and indulgence of him. With age, her love for Dad turned into some kind of dependency and complaints. When Dad was around, she couldn't stop complaining about what he did wrong. When he was not around, she couldn't stop worrying about his whereabouts and safety. Look, Grandma was at it again. Talking to herself, she started her scolding mantra, "Damn rascal! There are no traces of him anywhere. If you are manly, don't ever show up here again! I will have myself killed in front of you if you do!"

Rats from the kitchen drain scurried everywhere without fear, as if they knew that Dad was no longer here. Fat as they may be, these rats were able to carry themselves at a speed that

I could only dream about. Seeing them, most people could do nothing, but scream. But Dad was different. He would calmly raise his hand and slam it down fast to catch one. Its brain would be crushed when the rat was thrown down on the floor hard. Every time it happened, it would fill me with a sense of awe for Dad.

Shellac, our next-door neighbor, asked me, "Do you want to find your dad?" I said, "Of course, the number of rats in the drain is increasing fast." Shellac didn't get it right away. With two fingers elegantly clinching a cigar and another hand pressing his now famous glistening hairdo, he said, "Promise me you won't tell your dad and I will tell you. You look so miserable."

As I followed Shellac on a bicycle, I fancied that the femme fatale must live in a luxurious new building, wearing gold and silver and drinking Napoleon XO like the woman appeared in TV ads. In contrast, I ate cold box lunches in shivering cold weather. I was determined to call her a witch to her face in resentment.

"This non-local girl is thoroughly localized by now and is fluent in Shanghai dialect. She's quite glamorous. Stinky Bug is lucky with women, but not with money. His business is not doing that well, you know that, don't you?" said Shellac.

Shellac had a lot to drink that day and was quite talkative. He said that the femme fatale is from Sichuan. Just like the TV shows, she started out as an employee at Dad's store and then, "You know what happened afterwards." His description of the affair was straightforward and fuzzy. All the while, I wanted to smash something right there and then to express my anger.

Things turned out to be totally different. I found Dad in a small room in shantytown. Strangely, none of the things I fancied were here. The room was shabbily furnished and the wall was plastered with old calendar pictures, European city scenes mixed with night views of Shanghai. To me, the glittering night-lights of Shanghai were much more beautiful than the run-of-the-mill European sceneries. I would like to grow old and die here. I never need to leave Shanghai.

Things on the rickety table were few and simple, a rice cooker, an electric wok and a thermo. The layout of everything in the room gave you a temporary and patched-up feeling. I realized that it was not as pretty and comfortable as our home and the nearby housing was also a far cry from our alleyway. When I walked in, the femme fatale was sitting on a little stool cutting Dad's toenails. Dad was half-sitting in bed, playing with her long hair. I had never seen Mom and Dad ever get so intimate with each other. I also remembered vaguely that she was the good-hearted woman who sat next to me when Dad took me to dine at restaurants. It never occurred to me that she was the femme fatale. I stood there stunned wearing a stupid smile, like the smile I wore at two when I first saw the pigtail at Jianguo's place. I never uttered a harsh word, nor did I smash anything.

"Little Devil, how did you get here? Is Grandma ok?" Dad was shocked to see me there and his first question was about Grandma. That greeting shook me to the core. I remembered Grandma's words, "In the end, mother is always the person you feel closest to." Was it true? How would I feel about Mom later on in my life? Right now, she was becoming more and more disgusting. Her eyes were shadowed like a panda's and her face painted white. It was like "a real pasting" in white. In Chinese, the word *bai* could mean failure or white. Also, she didn't care for me. All she cared about was the house. I didn't want to let anyone know about this, especially Beibei and Wanwan. By the way, I was a fan of TV ads, and I was especially good at remembering the new use of old Chinese idioms by changing one character of the same pronunciation, such as: one needs to seize the opportunity (chicken), love at first sight (device), and marriage (gift box) that will last a hundred years.

"Grandma is alright. She just refuses to get out of bed. Dad, do you really want to give the house to her?" Instead of Mom, I surprised myself by using the pronoun "her."

"I was merely trying to scare Grandma. If I don't make any noise, do you think your mom will let me go? Now she knows that without Grandma's permission, there is nothing I can do about it!"

"In that case, I need to let Grandma know the truth so she will be at ease. Once her mind is at ease, she will get up and cook for me. Dad, I am tired of eating box lunches."

"Keep the truth away from Grandma. Hell, you have your lunch at school. Box lunch is only for supper. What is there to complain about? When I have time, I will come back and make dinner for you. Oh, call her Auntie." Dad responded with a frown. I was happy that he got distracted and forgot to ask me how I found my way there.

I reluctantly called the femme fatale "Auntie." I pretended not to remember her. The femme fatale tried to please me and stuffed a piece of candy into my mouth. Sure enough, she didn't look like someone from the countryside. She was clean, had fine features, and spoke with a soft, gentle and pleasant voice, like the mother of Wanwan. I tried hard to deny that she left a nice impression on me. After all, she was the other woman.

Wanwan said that she was determined to marry someone who was rich. She had no intention to continue her life in the alleyway, and would like to move to a house with a garden. I didn't think Dad was someone rich and couldn't understand why the femme fatale was willing to stay at such a shabby place.

"Grandma, I have been there and I saw her." The minute I said that, Grandma knew whom I was referring to.

"Little Devil, how did you find the place and what she looks like? What did your dad say to you?" Grandma sat up in bed, batting her eyes with excitement.

"He said he would return. You don't have to prepare for dinner any more. Dad will do it. As for her ..." I hesitated and held my tongue. At that moment, I somehow remembered the flavor of the candy she stuffed in my mouth.

"When did your dad become a man of his words? Like someone who spends three days fishing and two days drying nets, he will show up once in a while at most! As long as I am around, he knows that someone will pick up the slack. Would he have the heart to leave her? Wipe that stupid smile off your face, you miserable wretch. Just watch out for the fists of your stepmother. They are as terrible as the scorching sun in June!" Grandma warned, pouring cold water on me.

In fact, Shellac not only disclosed the femme fatale's place to me, but also to my mom. Shellac was angry at Dad. Rumor had it that both Mom and the femme fatale were his friends to begin with, but they later decided to go with Dad. In spite of this, Shellac and Dad were still on good terms.

Like me, Mom also found the small room Dad shared with the femme fatale. Mom saw that Dad was eating alone inside, the only dish he had was preserved vegetable. He was apparently not doing well.

"So, you are having a good time? Oh, hell, is that your son? When was the picture taken, at one or two? Tell me, where is the witch?" Mom checked every part of the room. Like a detective, she asked about the picture of a child under the glass sheet.

"Stop making trouble. This is a picture given to me by a friend. What are you doing here anyway?"

"I am here to ask for the same thing, the house."

"Forget about the house, you know very well that Mom will never let go of it. There is also Huazi. She is not an easy person to deal with. Her name is still on the household registry and she is sure to have a say on this."

"I think it was you who doesn't want to give it to me. What your mom feels is no concern to me. You just have to make it happen. I've asked around, and bigamy will lend you five years in jail. If you don't give me the house, you go to jail. You wimp!"

"You are the wimp! I am now waiting here for you to get the court people. Once I am in, I will be a free man. I no longer have to rush back and cook for Black Bug. Go have a life with your son."

"You are daydreaming. I don't want my son, nor will I have

anything to do with him in the future. It is you who did me wrong. The son is also the fault of yours. Why should I be held responsible for him?" she fired back at him.

"Well, if you don't want our son, why pressure me? The truth is that my business is not doing well. I've stopped renting the store space and I cannot afford a divorce. I don't want a divorce now. Just let it be. Let's all be cooked slowly like the making wheat paste."

"Is that what you have in mind? I want a divorce! I want the house! You blasted idiot, poisonous coffin! Fuck you! I will fight you with my life." Mom jumped up in a rage, hair in disarray, and threw herself at Dad.

"What's your problem? You're a lazy bitch and a piece of trash. You ruined my life. Get out!" Dragging Mom by her hair, Dad threw her out the door.

"Why don't you kill me? Go ahead and do it! I don't want to live …" Mom fell to the ground. She struggled to get up.

"If you take another half step, I will kill you! A life for a life!" Dad stared at her. His rectangular face turned livid. With his life apparently not going well, Dad was ready to risk it all.

Mom never dared to approach that small room again.

One day, two lawyers came to look for Grandma. They claimed that they were handling the divorce case at the request of Ms. Zhu, which is my Mom. Both were short in stature, one wore glasses with a mouth that stuck out and a chin like an ape's. The other one had big eyes and small ears. They both looked sharp. Upon learning that they were lawyers, Grandma grumbled, "He who has come is surely strong or he'd never have come along." The two lawyers pretended not to hear it.

"Old lady, do you know that your son committed bigamy?" The one with a mouth sticking out produced his ID at the request of Grandma and popped the question by pursing his lips in apparent displeasure.

"How would I know? My son is not a child. He is forty now.

I made sure that he studied and ate when he was young. As a grownup, I helped him get married and find a furnished room of his own, but I am not going to take care of him into his old age. I can't even if I wanted to. I am eighty years old, half of my body is already in earth. How many more years do I have?"

"According to law, bigamy is punishable by three to five years in prison. As a mother, are you going to sit there and let it happen?" With a serious look on his face, the small-eared lawyer was flipping the pages of a document in his hand, while restlessly shaking his legs.

"A man must bear the consequences of his own acts. If he indeed violated the law, what can I do about it? But, I am afraid that the fallout will affect not just him alone."

"You got it just right, old lady. You are an intelligent person, let's call a spade a spade. Right now, you have two options. You can put your signature down to satisfy the request of Ms. Zhu since she will need a place to stay after the divorce. If you do nothing, your son will languish in prison after Ms. Zhu files a case against him for bigamy."

"Bigamy is not something that can be established based on heresy. It needs hard proof. She can hire lawyers and so can we. A friend of my daughter is the owner of a law firm. The family of this black-hearted woman owns a house much bigger than ours. Why is it necessary for her to stay at this wretched tiny apartment? You people just take a look. This is the only decent room we have and this is her room now. My son, my grandson, and I are squeezed into the small attic. Is this a reasonable arrangement? You tell me. Even a beggar mother will always have a soft spot for her son who is a well-to-do official. Why is it that this women doesn't seem to care about her own son?"

"Ms. Zhu had no choice, but to give up her son. She doesn't have a regular job and has nowhere to raise a child. Of course, you will have problems, but you can work it out. Your son and your grandson can find a rental somewhere. As for Ms. Zhu, how can a married daughter move back in with her parents?" The small-eared lawyer's legs were shaking so hard that I worried that he might fall off his chair.

"First, you tried to force me to sign off on the property, and then you tried to put my son out in the street. I am not going to agree to that! The one who files the case first is not always the one who is in the right. I am prepared to fight it out with her in court. Don't you try to take advantage of an old lady. I have my legitimate rights, too. As to married daughters, the divorced married daughters of our alleyway are all back live with their parents. I don't go out much, but I watch TV every day. People also drop by constantly, so I know the new rules!"

"We have no intention to force your hand. Ms. Zhu is a victim in this marriage and we usually provide more care and support to the victim. After all, laws are tools for justice. Your son is the one who is in the wrong. Aside from giving up the house, he may have to pay some monetary damages as well. If you refuse to let Ms. Zhu have the house, we will support Ms. Zhu's lawsuit against your son. By then, old lady, your good lawyer is not going to make any difference. You may end up losing both the house and your son," said the lawyer with the protruding mouth forcefully with spit flying all over.

"You are just trying to scare me, In fact, like the blind eating wontons—you know very well how many you've had. You know for a fact that she is not going to file the complaint in court."

"Why?" said both lawyers.

"What will she gain by filing? Like doing a somersault in the hole of a coin, the black-hearted woman is money crazy. All she cares about is the house and money! If her husband is in jail, she will not receive a cent. She would have to raise their boy on her own, and she will turn out to be the loser. Is she ready to risk that?"

The two lawyers were stumped for a change.

I was hiding behind the door and hadn't missed a word of the exchanges. Grandma was indeed glib and quick-tongued in argument and the lawyers Mom hired were lousy in comparison.

I felt sorry for Mom, although I didn't want her to get the house.

I didn't want to leave the house. I have lived in for so long. There was this rancid and warm feeling to it. I sometimes woke up in the middle of the night and heard wild cats making their way to the terrace upstairs. They would madly chase each other up and down the stairway at great speed. I could understand how they relished this joy and freedom. I am running with them in my dream as well.

At day break, there would be calls for Old Shandong one after another from the back alleyway. Everyone before going to work or school, would want a bowl of small wonton. I would get up amid Grandma's loud hollering. By the time I stood in the back alleyway brushing my teeth, Old Shandong would be soliciting our business at our doorstep.

"Good morning, young gentleman. Two *liang*s (1 *liang* equals to 0.05 kg) of small wonton?"

"More soup! More filling inside!"

"For an old customer, sure!" Old Shandong nodded at me smiling.

I also liked to wonder around the alleyway on bicycle like a fish swimming in water, where every turn was a temptation enticing me to take a risk. I especially enjoyed hearing the ring of the St. Francis grand clock. Its sound was solemn and long lasting, tolling that way for more than a hundred years. It is a symbol of the past, the present, and the future.

I loved our alleyway and our house, during the day and at night.

After the visit of the protruding mouth and small-eared lawyers, Grandma started the process of getting Zhimin, the daughter of Meizi, residency in Shanghai. I found out that Grandma was actually stubborn on the outside, but soft inside. Someone who didn't mean what she said at times.

"Meizi had a hard time during her days in the countryside. Once I get Zhimin's application approved, I will have no more regrets in life." Grandma confessed to the sisters of her age group in our neighborhood.

Grandma had many such sisters in the alleyway. They looked like a tight-knit group, but they would each go their separate ways when the time came. Take the grandma of Jiajia for example, known as "Laolao" in the alleyway. Like Old Shandong, Laolao had been running a business without a license for many years. Old Shandong was making wontons while Laolao was making frying cakes. Others said that Laolao had saved a lot of money on the side. Grandma and Laolao had been members of the same neighborhood sewing group. They were good friends who got together often to hang out and gossip. But one time, Grandma lost money in playing mahjong and hard pressed, she borrowed 150 yuan from Laolao. Ever since then, Laolao would drop in at our place every day.

"Laolao, I suppose you are afraid that I will die suddenly and no one will be held responsible for the 150 yuan that I owe you. I know that I'm no good to you dead. Here, let me give you an IOU note," Grandma finally said one day.

"That kind of talk is totally uncalled for. We are like old sisters. Is it wrong for me to pop in and see how you are doing? Ok, Ok, I will leave. What a fool I am! Your heart must have been eaten by dogs." Laolao on the defensive left the scene in a hurry.

"No more loans beyond the age of seventy, the ancients were right on that one. Laolao went too far this time, she looked down on me as a person. After all, I have children who are accomplished, established and doing well, I am just not used to asking them for money." Her pride hurt, Grandma asked Huazi for the cash to immediately settle the loan with Laolao. Since then, Huazi became firmly against Grandma's return to her glory days at the mahjong table.

The procedures involved for Zhimin's return were very complex. With unsteady steps, Grandma ran from neighborhood offices to district offices seeking advice, making registrations, and enlisting the help of others. Once there was news, she would call Meizi long-distance.

"You need to make a trip to Shanghai. There is still no news about Zhimin's school transfer. The district office has stated clearly that you need to send everything in before August, and they will allow for no exceptions," she spoke with an imposing tone, choosing her words carefully, as if she were the district official in charge. I noticed that she used entirely different tones when talking to Huazi and Meizi.

"I will be there. I will take the leave and be there right away," Meizi promised without questioning.

With Zhimin's household and school registration documentation in tow, Meizi made many trips between Shanghai and Hefei. On every trip, Meizi would bring a lot of peanuts and wild fiddlehead fern with her. She said that those things cost her nothing since she was in charge of the canteen's warehouse.

The first night of Meizi's return, she had a long talk with Grandma in the attic. Her narrow and sharp-edged voice came out exceptionally clear, like a long, bright light cutting across the dark night. Grandma was even more excited than Meizi, she talked about what the family had been through. Like untangling a jumble of memories, there were no order, no beginning, and no end. Grandma first touched on the subject of the absence of Dad in the last couple of months. She then went back to the days when Dad was given a hard beating by the Red Guard activists. In the midst of her story, Grandma broke down and cried.

"The last one of our line. Dogs must have eaten up his conscience. The short-lived lawyers tried to use his possible five-year sentence to scare me off. I told them that a man should answer for what he does himself. I wouldn't lose any sleep over that case if it really happens … You should have seen how he tried to have his way with me. He was ready to eat me up. He threw my teacup to the ground. Here, just like this …" Grandma imitated the crackling sound in the attic.

Lying in the bedroom downstairs, I tried to imagine Grandma's spot on impersonation of Dad. I knew that from then on, the story of the teacup would become classic family lore.

"My goodness! None of our family members have ever acted like that, right? When we fought, the most I would do was talk back. Mom, I am a little scared of Stinky Bug, too. He has this air of truculence about him. I remembered that he used to come home bloody all over from group fighting ... Mommy, I am so moved that you are not holding my past mistakes against me. I really miss you a lot not being around," said Meizi as she wept. Meizi was an emotional woman. Her gratitude, anger, pain and joy were always expressed through waterworks.

Amid the sobbing exchanges between Grandma and Meizi, I got drowsy and fell asleep. I dreamt that my desk mate was picking on me. She was a female bully. Every time my arm crossed the 38th parallel line, she would nudge and poke me with a pointed pencil. I remembered Dad's admonition: this world is full of violence and deceit. An idea suddenly crossed my mind, so I raised my hand and told the teacher that I couldn't concentrate in class because she kept talking to me. The teacher took the bait and expelled her from class, and heaped praise on me for being honest and courageous. Hearing the girl's cry for being wronged, I was overwhelmed by my own feeling of triumph.

Daylight was already here by the time I woke up amid the girl's crying. I was surprised to hear the sobbing of Meizi and Grandma in the attic. Not yet fully awake, I wasn't sure if I was in the classroom of my dream or in bed at home. I was a little confused. Had they cried through the night until now?

Meizi always regarded herself as a Shanghai native. She said that she was always immediately recognized as Shanghainese wherever she went in Hefei.

To me, Meizi was more like pure country folk. She sounded uncivilized, had a dark skin tone, and dressed on the gaudy side. Huazi on the other hand was slim, fair, beautiful, and dressed elegantly. Meizi also spoke with a strange drawl that sounded exaggerated and funny. She could no longer speak the pure Shanghai dialect.

Meizi also had a nickname: Sour Plum. When they were small, Meizi and Dad always mocked each other by endlessly screaming the other's nickname, Stinky Bug and Sour Plum.

Meizi was also very short. She didn't look like someone from the same family as Dad and Huazi. Huazi often joked that Grandma took Meizi home as a result of a hospital mix-up. Grandma's version was different. She attributed Meizi's height from going to the countryside at the age of 16. Meizi tried to dodge hard labor, but had to carry heavy loads from time to time. This led to her stunted growth.

I took Meizi to see Dad. Meizi had peanuts and wild fiddlehead fern with her. As we left home, we didn't dare to tell Grandma where we were going. Grandma was lying in bed then, and then we heard her kicking a bag at the end of the bed. Apparently, she wanted to say something. We had to hold our steps.

"Take this to the rascal!" She then turned her back towards us and never said another word.

When we opened the bag outside, we saw clothes and two packs of Zhonghua cigarettes for Dad. At the sight of these things, Meizi cried again.

Meizi went to see Dad mostly for her daughter Zhimin. She worried that Dad would not like to have Zhimin around. She figured that the reason why Grandma worked so hard for Zhimin's return probably had something to do with her fight with Dad.

"Pure speculation. Don't you think I know Mom's temper? It is true that she is mad at me. It is also true that she did all of that for you. I may not be home, but I am sure of all that. Hell, it is possible that Mom is worried about the house and she means to frustrate that bitch. Once Zhimin is added to the household registry, it would be even more difficult for that bitch to lay a finger on the house." Eating the peanuts with his fingers, Dad clapped his hands.

"Once Zhimin is in Shanghai, I hope you as her uncle would look after her."

"Why do you talk like that? Where did you learn such Japanese etiquette? Her return to Shanghai is in agreement with government policy. Why would I oppose it? Rest assured, I am okay with it."

"With those words, I am really relieved. I've heard many cases of troubled relationships between the uncle and aunt, and the children of the educated youths as they stay with their grandma after returning to Shanghai. Some of them even ended in killings. Of course, I don't mean to imply anything. I wanted to take a leave and come with her, but the work unit denied my request. I have also asked others to help out, but to no avail. I have not clarified the matter with Mom. Now I can only ask you for help to take care of my daughter ..."

"Don't underestimate me. We both have been to the countryside. You went to work in the fields and I was in a farm. It's six of one and half a dozen of the other, we all had our misfortunes. I will help out even on that score alone."

"In that case, should I mail you her living expenses? Even brothers need to keep their accounts clear."

"As for living expenses, if you want to mail it, mail it to Mom. I would not take even one cent from you. If I eat rice, Zhimin will not have to settle for soupy rice. If I have meat, Zhimin will not settle for dried turnip!"

"You are a good man, Stinky Bug. If you ever come to Hefei, I will certainly treat you with nice wine. In Shanghai, I am no match to you people. I am merely a poor soul from Anhui. But back in my factory in Hefei, I am really doing well. I have tasted dainties of every kind and tried a variety of game meat. Although I live in a one level house, I managed to install a bathroom with a flushing toilet three years ago. Many people in my factory came to look at it with envy. They marveled at how we people from Shanghai knew how to enjoy life! Once I am back in Shanghai, I don't have the sense of superiority anymore. Look at you, even the water you drink is treated water. I am an unsophisticated country bumpkin in comparison …"

"Don't you think I am in the same boat as you? I'm cramped in a small space and live from day-to-day. In spite of the smart western suit I am in, the Zhonghua brand cigarettes I smoke, and the treated water I drink, I am a man who earned his own living! I need to ask others for favors. For renting a store space, I had to take care of the people from the business bureau, the tax bureau, and the environment office. It is so difficult. Just take a look at Huazi. She works for a public enterprise with a car and a house. The apartment allocated to her is worthy of at least 500,000 yuan. For me to have that kind of money, I'd have to rob a bank! Everybody is different …"

"You are right. Quite right. I think everybody's fate is predetermined. Huazi certainly looked no different from us before. She is just lucky. I have it all figured out. All my hopes are now pinned on my daughter. I hope she will make it. I believe that I will have a better life in my old age, probably a life that can match Huazi … Oh, you promised that you would cook for Street Runner, but I heard that you did it only once and didn't speak to Mom at all the whole time. I think you should let it go. After all, she is your own mom. What's the point of holding a grudge against her? Look, here are the things Mom asked me to bring to you. These suits are for your business needs, right?" Meizi opened up the package and took out the clothing piece by piece for Dad to check.

"Put them away. As for Mom, I have a very good idea about her situation. Judging from how she looked, she seemed to be all right. I need to make a trip to deliver some goods that will take a few days. After it is done, I will see how she's been doing back home. Tell Mom that if she can't manage, just give 10 yuan to Street Runner to get something to eat from the stores and I will settle the account with her later."

The conversation between Meizi and Dad was quite

straightforward, devoid of hypocrisy and niceties. This was our family tradition. In a few exchanges, they settled on affairs with Zhimin, and my affairs as well. From then on, I nagged Grandma for 10 yuan every day. For that small fortune, I would rather that Grandma stayed in bed all day.

I started expecting the arrival of Zhimin.

Zhimin finally arrived in Shanghai in summer. All of a sudden I had an older sister under the same roof.

By the time she came, Mom and Dad were already divorced. But Mom still lived with us. She didn't get what she wanted the most—the house, but she got a huge sum of money to compensate. She said that without the money, she would've never agreed to move out without a fuss. At that time, Grandma was too old to negotiate the stairs, and her diabetes also flared up often. After Mom and Dad argued for three days and three nights, Mom finally moved into Grandma's quarter in the attic after Dad used her monetary compensation as a threat. My 80-year-old Grandma finally returned to a room downstairs.

Zhimin looked somewhat like Huazi. Her skin tone was also fair, but she was smaller in size. Probably the result of Meizi's genes. She was four years older than me.

One small bed was added to the room downstairs. It had a metal frame and a wood plank, emitting a sweet smell of the mixed material. Truly a lovely sight. It was especially made for Zhimin, but I beat her to it by being there first. So the next day when Zhimin arrived, she ended up sharing a bed with Grandma.

Feeling a little guilty for taking her bed away, I went out of my way to show my hospitality.

"Sister!" I shouted at Zhimin. The first time that word came out of my mouth, I had this delighted feeling that my whole heart was about to take flight. I had never called my cousin Xiaoli this affectionately before. Taken by surprise, Grandma looked at me and twitched her mouth disapprovingly.

"This morning, the sun came out from the west. Zhimin, just

call him Black Bug Street Runner." Grandma introduced me to Zhimin, imitating the tone of a TV host introducing his guests. I was probably nitpicking, but I noticed that Grandma's mandarin had a very strong accent. It was particular to people from the northern part of Jiangsu Province, similar to the cab driver with a crooked nose. No wonder it became an issue with Meizi.

Zhimin was hesitating, she naturally found it hard to address me by my nickname as a new comer. She kept silent for quite a while with pursed lips. I got embarrassed and finally said, "My name is Gu Longfei." At the suggestion of Huazi, Zhimin cut the first and third characters of my name off and called me "Longlong." I thus gained another nickname. I experienced a whole new feeling when hearing her call me by that name. It seemed like everything in the household, including the attic, had brightened up. I tried hard to do well and impress her. But the harder I tried, the goofier I seemed.

As I took her hand into mine, I gave her a tour from the front to the back of the house. I pointed out to Zhimin which water tap was ours, which broken wash basin could serve as a stand-in garbage bin, how to turn on and off the gas, what to do if the water closet in the bathroom started leaking, and how to tell the face basin and foot basin apart. Our house would never be classified as high-class, but we did have a gas supply and our own bath. We heard that more than half a century ago, a Japanese businessman lived in this home. He's responsible for the Japanese style squatting flushed toilet, the shoji windows, and the gas stove. The toilet and the now blackened gas stove represented the legacy from that era. Only after I grew up, did I come to realize that some of the Hongkou District of Shanghai today was once the Japanese concession. It turned out that the layout of our house was the leftover of a loathsome Japanese custom.

Meizi accompanied Zhimin to Shanghai, and said that she could only stay for three days at most before returning to Hefei. Grandma was stunned by the news.

"Didn't you tell me originally that you could take a leave of absence? How can I manage without you? Street Runner is an exception. With him, my hands are already full. The neighbors would disapprove if I let go of him. I have no more energy to spare for Zhimin. When my diabetes flares up, I can hardly take care of myself. Huazi and others do not take my problem seriously. Like a clay Buddha fording the river, I can hardly save myself now."

"I have already told Stinky Bug my situation and he promised to help out. With business booming, the factory has abolished the leave of absence policy. If I insist, I would be let go, along with my fringe benefits and medical insurance. After over twenty years of hard work and retirement imminent, I have no choice, but to bite the bullet till the end."

"You are all busy. Only this old lady with a full belly is twiddling her thumbs all day? You know that Stinky Bug is unreliable. He only comes home once in a blue moon to bring some groceries and make dinner, while I am getting weaker by the day. I can only make a vegetable dish, an egg drop soup, and maybe two more fried eggs at most. I am doing the best I can. I can't make it to the market anymore."

"Whatever you eat is fine with Zhimin. Worse comes to worst just ask her to buy a box lunch. Mom, I am really sorry about this. Just hang in there for two more years. I will jump on every opportunity to come back." Meizi is someone who is open to persuasion, but not to coercion. She didn't leave any room for negotiation and returned to Hefei.

I am a people person by nature, which is my biggest selling point. I soon was on good terms with Zhimin. To my regret, Mom treated Zhimin like a total stranger. She probably shouldn't be blamed for it. After all, no one ever told Zhimin how to address my Mom. Mom no longer had any relation with the family members, except me. They didn't even acknowledge each other when meeting face to face. Then I noticed that Zhimin took extra care and caution in her approach to Mom. Maybe because Meizi had already told her the whole story. Fortunately, Mom was a night person, chances of her ever encountering Zhimin were extremely rare.

Because of my engaging personality, Zhimin became dependent on me, especially since her relationship with Grandma wasn't that smooth after Meizi left. She only had me as a close friend.

Before Meizi left, she had a fight with Grandma, and it was all my fault.

Ever since the arrival of Zhimin, I had been in a state of high excitement. Understandably, I wasn't always on my best behavior. For instance, I was unusually boisterous in an attempt to show off and I refused to heed to Meizi's admonition. She was not as generous, sophisticated, and well-rounded like Huazi. She was the family member who was taken least seriously by others.

Meizi intended to establish authority over me.

On that day, Grandma began counting with pride all the things Huazi and Jianguo bought for the family, including the TV and the microwave. She then turned her praises to Dad. She said it was true that Dad could be tempestuous sometimes, but even the daughters were no match to him when he put his mind to something. Grandma cited the way in which Dad would give up his bamboo lounge chair to her when we were outside enjoying the cool evening breezes in the summer. He would always remember to wipe the chair with a cool towel first, so that she wouldn't feel the discomfort of sitting on the leftover warmth of others.

"The feeling you get on a bamboo lounge chair that was wiped with a cool towel is so refreshing, even better than air conditioning," Grandma exaggerated.

When the subject turned to the uncle in Beijing, Grandma waxed eloquent about his busy schedule and his extreme importance to show off. Grandma had praised all her children except Meizi. Meizi stayed silent, not making a peep.

Later, Meizi somehow started talking about men and women. Meizi said, "To me all men are rotten, not satisfied with what they have in their bowls, they miss the things in the pot. Not satisfied with having a wife, they want to have lovers." She pointed her fingers at me and said, "Your dad is rotten, too!" I had never heard Dad being so criticized by others. Honestly, even Grandma's endless tirade against Dad never angered me, but Meizi's words truly drove me over the edge.

I fired back, "You are the one who is rotten! You are the sour plum, Sour Plum!"

"Did you just use my nickname? This is outrageous, a mere child is trying to disparage me, where is your manners?"

"Sour Plum! Sour Plum!"

"If you say it again, I won't go easy on you. I will spank you!"

"Ok, ok, I've had enough of your fighting! Meizi, you haven't visited for a long while. How could you be so hard on him?" Grandma made her move.

"Mom, you heard him. Street Runner is an unruly child. His mom and dad could care less and you people don't seem to care either. I am his aunt. I can set him straight and make sure that he behaves!"

"If you want to talk the talk, walk the walk first. He always behaves in front of Huazi. Huazi couldn't bear the thought of laying a finger on him. She treasures Street Runner as much as her own life. Can't you just be nicer to him?"

"Don't you cover up for him! You all look down on me, and now even the child knows it. He is behaving this way because of your backing!"

"You idiot! I tried to stop you from quarreling and you, like Pigsy Zhu Bajie (a character in the *Journey to the West*), turned around and hit me with a rake. You accused me of covering up for Black Bug, so I will. Don't you dare hit Street Runner!"

"I am his aunt. Why can't I set him straight? Children need to behave, or who knows what will happen."

"Well, you just can't. I am here today. If you want to hit him, hit me first! I dare you! You want to lay down the rules for him? I will lay down rules for you."

"You really pissed me off today. You're trying to take me down because you look down on me. I am poor and Hefei's wages are low. If I had the money, I could also afford to be generous. If I bought a microwave and the TV for you, and surprised Street Runner with something delicious and interesting, would you have nice words for me then? I don't have the economic means. And you despise me just because I don't."

"Are you blaming me now? Hell, what did I do wrong? I went through the process of getting residency for your daughter. I showered people with gifts in return for the favor. Have I ever asked you for even one cent? My feet hurt, and I limped around to get to all these offices here and there for Zhimin's sake. Did I do wrong? Like Awang's sticky rice cake, everyone enjoys it, but no one appreciates the efforts that went into it. And now you are trying to break my heart. Huazi is good, Jianguo is also good. Whatever you say, I will insist that they are good."

"I am not going to argue with you. I may be poor, but I am not poor in spirit. So long as I have a clear conscience, I am fine with it. Every time I come to Shanghai, not only do I lose pay for my days away from work, there are other expenses together that almost cost me a whole year's of savings. All of this for the sake of seeing how you—my mom—are doing. But no one ever appreciated my efforts ..." Meizi started crying. I found out that Meizi and Grandma were definitely both hardheaded and were wrong for each other.

While Meizi was crying, Zhimin bit her lip and stood close by her mother's side in silence. Her eyes welled up with tears. That was probably the moment Zhimin started keeping her distance from Grandma.

Zhimin had a soft voice and was not talkative. Grandma didn't like Zhimin, she said Zhimin's voice was "soft like a mosquito." But I liked it very much. Our heads would touch whenever I talked to her. I could smell the fresh scent of Zhimin's shampoo as well as the sweet and tangy after-meal breath from her mouth.

After Meizi left, Zhimin started sharing a bed with Grandma.

They were indeed strange bedfellows. Grandma was obsessed day and night with Dad who spent his nights away from home. While Zhimin missed her mom Meizi. Zhimin was fifteen at the time. Meizi always said Zhimin was a child, but Grandma would counter that a 15-year-old was no longer a child. Grandma was especially upset at the fact that Meizi would telephone several times a week and would exchange in embarrassingly coquettish talks with Zhimin.

"Chickabiddy, you hang up first."

"You first."

"Alright, a kiss for you, (sounds of tongue clicking) ..."

"Another one please ..."

This kind of nonsense on the telephone would go on for quite some time between Meizi and Zhimin. Sometimes Zhimin would even tear up after she hung up. Like her mother, Zhimin was a girl prone to crying. Every time Zhimin cried, Grandma would react in a huff with her lips twisted and her face ashen.

Finally Grandma had enough. She asked for Huazi's telephone number and complained bitterly.

"This idiotic Meizi telephones five times a week. She claimed that she was short on money. How come she doesn't feel the pain when burning money on long distance calls?"

"Mom, she misses her daughter. This is human nature. Just let it go. After all, you are not the one paying for the calls."

"Human nature? In the last eight years, I never heard a word from her. She never placed a telephone call to me. Did she ever miss me, her own mother? And now, the daily call is meant for her daughter! With me, she just had a few words of a routine nature. Like the monks reciting scriptures, they are repeating something they don't mean. Her remarks to me were mostly perfunctory! I have nothing much to say to her either!"

"Meizi went to the countryside at the age of sixteen. People didn't have telephones at home then. Didn't you force me to write to her every day and cry your heart out? You forgot that? Zhimin is not yet sixteen. Just let it go and don't think too much of it."

"Bullshit! Where did Meizi go then? And what place has Zhimin ended up with now? Shanghai and the countryside are as different as a pompadour and a mangy head. How can these two places be mentioned in the same breath? This idiot, I was making things right before and now this is the trouble that has come upon me. I should have known!"

"How is the girl?" Huazi changed the subject and asked about Zhimin. But the new subject proved to be even more explosive.

"Literally, nice as hell! She is particular about food and very picky. She won't touch leftovers and doesn't eat vegetables. If there's a shrimp dish and braised pork in brown sauce on the table, she would only eat those dishes. As the saying goes, you fit your appetite to the dishes, but in her case, it is just the opposite. She has no table manners to speak of. Another strange thing, the girl only washes her own bowl, minding her own business."

"Why don't you say something? She's still a kid who doesn't know how to behave properly and you are the grandma."

"I can't. If Meizi found out I said something, she would think that I was abusing her precious daughter. I want her to come back. How could she leave her daughter here and wash her hands of it?"

"She really had no choice, pressuring her is not going to make any difference. I have a meeting coming, I have to go now. Just relax and stay out of their business. Let them do as they please ..."

"Ok, I'll stay out of their business ... Huazi, I have to tell you that my feet are again swollen. My diabetes is flaring up again and I have no energy. Please bring me some medicine."

"Ok. Mom, please stop saying that something is flaring up again. If your feet are swollen, don't work too hard and rest properly. I will drop by to see you when I have time." Huazi hung up the phone in a hurry.

"Every time the subject of my flaring-up comes up, she tries to avoid it like the plague. The usual appearance of caring for others is just a façade." Staring at the busy-signaled receiver, Grandma grumbled and sighed. I only realized later that although Grandma called Huazi for help every time she felt the need, she was actually deeply disappointed at Huazi.

Nevertheless, we were most happy when Huazi would come to visit. Huazi would always bring a little something not only to me, but also to Zhimin. Huazi was someone who cared about her image. At the end of her visits, Zhimin and I would always walk her to the alleyway entrance and see her get into a taxi and disappear into the flow of traffic. I would then take Zhimin to wander in the streets and lanes, from the hospital to the railroad station, to all the bustling places that once so fascinated me. I wanted to share all these with Zhimin. To my regret, the Triangle Market place now laid in ruins, and a modern commercial building would replace it. At a tender age, I saw with my own eyes the great changes that would come with time.

"Street Runner, you only pretend to see Aunt Huazi off. Your real intention is to go out and have a good time. You think I don't know what lousy ideas are in your head?" One day, Zhimin and I walked Huazi out as usual only to see Grandma blocking our way at the alleyway entrance. She was so pleased to have caught me in one of my tricks.

I tittered in embarrassment.

"Black Bug, you've got a 'sister' and will soon get an 'auntie,' the 'she' in your Dad's life. You are lucky with women." Grandma deliberately imitated my titter. Grandma had a peculiar sense of humor. When she was in the mood, she would come up with a string of strange nonsense.

Huazi who was about to get into the cab, hearing how Grandma mocked me, shook her head. "Mom, no wonder Street Runner makes things difficult for you. Just look at you, spreading rumors with no consideration to the fact that you are not of the same generation as Street Runner. As I said long time ago, you and Street Runner, you get along, you fight, it's a matter between you two, there is no point for anyone else to get involved."

Trying to suppress a smile she then added, "Street Runner, are you happy now that you are lucky with women? You owe it to your sex appeal!"

As I said before, Huazi talked much boldly and freely once she was back home. I made a face at Huazi.

"Bye-bye!" Huazi waved from inside the car. She looked so lovely that it reminded me of the days before she got married. She used to hold me in her arms and we rolled in bed.

Grandma always gave Zhimin a hard time. Grandma would raise no objection when I did certain things, but all hell would break lose if Zhimin did those same things. Being picky with food, dish washing after dinner, or going out to play were just a few examples. Aside from worrying about my safety, Grandma never got angry with me when I went out and did crazy things day and night. But Zhimin would not be this lucky. Grandma was especially angry when Zhimin went to visit Beibei upstairs.

Beibei from upstairs was a one-track minded girl. She always brought a lot of homework back home, but she was not doing any better than me. I was a repeater because I spent too much time playing and didn't do my exercises. Zhimin was in a higher grade. She first went to visit Beibei because she got to eat the yogurt she loved most there. Later on, Zhimin became an unpaid tutor for Beibei.

Zhimin's visit was warmly received by Beibei's father Little Missy. He once forbade me to spend time with Beibei. In contrast, he now kept an ample supply of yogurt from the supermarket at home for Zhimin. And after Zhimin finished her tutoring, Little Missy was also kind enough to allow Zhimin to play on his computer. Zhimin was taking a computer class after school, so like a fish in water, she really enjoyed her stays there.

I didn't like going to Beibei's place because we were required to keep our voices down and our behavior in check. Her father always sized me up critically and harshly, trying to suppress my rambunctious nature. I became a "trouble maker" ever since I was four or five when Beibei followed my example and broke her shinbone while jumping from stand to stand in the vegetable market. He also assumed an air of an educated gentleman. Grandma told me that he always spitted in front of other people's homes as a boy. After careful observation, I indeed caught him throwing garbage from upstairs while no one was paying attention. No wonder I often found peels and rinds wrapped in unused financial spreadsheets on the stones lining up the alleyway.

Grandma had no kind words for Zhimin when she sat in the back alleyway chitchatting with Laolao, Old Shandong, and others.

"You all can serve as my witnesses. The girl never acknowledged or spoke to anyone of her comings and goings. Her eyes are on top of her head and her lips have been sealed."

"What's wrong with Meizi? How could she leave her daughter behind in Shanghai like this, ditching her as if she were dead?"

"She is making big money in Hefei! Humph, 300 yuan a month, even a garbage collector makes more than that in Shanghai! She is afraid that she will have to take care of an old bag like me. As I said a long time ago, once I croak I don't want anyone of my children to show up! Or they will be shamed by everybody in the alleyway." Grandma was always in a bad mood when talking about Meizi. She firmly believed that Meizi was trying to shirk her responsibility.

"Haven't you heard about the Huang family at 21 of the alleyway? Her granddaughter like Zhimin, is also the child of the educated youths who went to the countryside. She comes from Yunnan and she's a real character. Once her grandma scolded her over something, she had it surreptitiously recorded and played it to her mom when she visited. Distraught at the treatment of her daughter, the mother had a big fight with the grandma. Exasperated, the grandma could only respond with well, well ..."

"This is why I keep my mouth shut. I will just watch, I am not going to ask for embarrassment. Laolao, through the help of others, I managed to buy six pieces of spare ribs yesterday. Then these two nuisances swooped them all up. I didn't even taste the ribs, I had to settle for vegetable soup. The girl lacks good manners, and has no love and devotion for the older generation. One day, Meizi will be the one to suffer, not me."

"Just let it go, they are all your flesh and blood. Maternal grandchildren are no different from paternal ones."

"Do you know how much money Meizi gives me every month? How can a poor old lady like me afford to raise another child with the money she gives me? With Black Bug, I have no choice, like a wet hand that has already touched the flour ... The strange thing is that Black Bug follows her everywhere like a shadow. In the past few nights, the girl has been staying upstairs a lot. Once gossip flies around and causes problems, it will be too late. Alas, you should see how restless Black Bug becomes when he is home alone, just like a headless fly."

When Zhimin came back from school that day, I secretly accosted her at the alleyway entrance. "Sister, Grandma again trashes you in front of the people in the alleyway ..." I then repeated everything I heard to Zhimin, since I wished to help her out. I also fancied that Zhimin would probably keep her distance from Beibei as a result. Little did I expect that Zhimin would become even more reticent towards Grandma and increase the frequency of her visits upstairs.

I would stay home when Zhimin went upstairs for Beibei. Even if I went out to play, I wouldn't dare to go far in case Zhimin needed me. I would wait anxiously for her return. And Grandma would be especially angry at seeing me in that state and mock me maliciously.

"Street Runner, are you ready to enlist in the army? Why hurry home so soon? Is there a devil waiting for you?" That night, I had asked One Bamboo to go playing video games with me, but I stepped into a puddle at the club entrance. Both of my shoes immediately filled with water like riverboats, so I ran home to change my shoes when Grandma greeted me with those snide remarks.

"What's wrong with the devil? I like the devil!"

"I am afraid the feeling is not mutual. The devil has no intention of being close to you."

"There is no need for you to be so sarcastic and mean. I am not to talk to you. I am here to change my shoes."

"I was telling you a fact. Don't you think I know? You stay home alone every day and she has long forgotten about you upstairs. Why don't you plead to her in your special endearing way?" In an exaggerated manner, Grandma imitated the way I called "sister."

In exasperation, instead of changing shoes, I stomped feverishly on Grandma's bed with my dirty shoes, screaming and yelling at the same time.

"So you let your frustration out on me? Have I ever mistreated you? If you were a child with a conscience, dogs would not eat shit!" Grandma barked at me and slapped me on the face. This was the first time that Grandma ever laid her hands on me.

I felt my cheek and came face to face with Grandma. We both calmed down unexpectedly. Getting slapped somehow gave me a sense of security. Grandma's quivering lips had confirmed her love for me. I didn't get upset about being hit. I never held any grudges against Dad for viciously beating me.

I was a wretch who deserved to be punished.

One day after school, I discovered that Mom had disappeared from our home. The down comforter, the wool blanket, and Mom's clothing in the closet were all gone. She left without saying anything to me. I looked around the room, her beautiful picture under the glass sheet was no longer there, along with her lipsticks, lotions, and her blonde hair dye. I couldn't find anything that belonged to Mom. In a frenzy, I rushed to the attic hoping that she was still up there. I wanted so badly to see her sleeping soundly as usual, with flocks of hair on her yellowish cheeks like the cloth doll Beibei ditched in the corner of the room upstairs.

Mom wasn't in the attic, I sat in silence on the cluttered floor. Downstairs, Grandma was watching TV. A commercial was promoting a skincare product, "… For a child, a mother's hands are the most tender …" I knew that Mom would leave me one day and be gone forever. I then remembered the term "broken family" mentioned often on TV. Now our family was indeed "broken." But everything seemed to be the same, and life went on. As usual, Grandma still watched TV in bed, Dad was having a good time with the femme fatale, and I was still obsessed with the 10 yuan in my pocket—my daily allowance to cover breakfast, dinner, plus beverages and snacks. In order to save money for video games, I didn't have breakfast that day. In the video world, I commanded a great number of people and had also killed a large number of people, and the exhilaration it gave me was simply ethereal.

As I sat alone in the attic, I didn't feel the sadness and desperation that comes with a "broken family" since my mind was preoccupied by video games. I learned at a very young age that family was a disparate unit to begin with, and that was our way of existence. I only had a sense of loss, I'd rather that Mom was still in the attic, sleeping during the day. It almost felt like she died. I didn't think Mom had any real significance in my life, but her existence was at least some kind of capital that allowed me to stay proudly in the ranks of children with two parents. There were many single parent children in my class. Once on Children's Day, the teacher asked all of them to step up and gave all of them an extra gift on the side in a show of kindness. I didn't want to be included in their ranks, which to me was a public disgrace. I also had no desire to stand up there holding a cheap gift with a stupid smile.

More importantly, the existence of Mom allowed me to face the gloating Beibei, Wanwan, Little Black skin, and One Bamboo with equanimity. The funny thing is, the only thing they could show off in front of me were their mothers, although they sometimes hated their mothers to the bone.

Dad came too into my mind. With Mom gone, I fancied that Dad might dote on me and love me more because I was a motherless child. I learned later that Dad was busy preparing for his move back home that day. He had long looked forward to the day when he and the femme fatale could leave that shantytown behind. I felt that Dad's behavior seemed too anxious for his own good.

In the days afterwards, I still managed to have a wild and great time. But on the day Mom left home, I did feel something was amiss. The image of her sound asleep haunted me. I figured that she must have gotten the money she wanted and would never come back to see me again. To be honest, her lofty stance of giving up on me had left me feeling dejected. I'd rather that she and Dad would fight over my guardianship.

At that time, Zhimin was my best friend. She stayed with me the whole evening, without going to Beibei's. In my mind, Zhimin had long replaced all the women in my life: Mom, Huazi, Grandma, Wanwan ... That night, Zhimin and I played chess. I hadn't touched the pieces for a long time. And I remembered what the two old men playing chess said to me during my crazy days at the vegetable market, they asked, "Gee, don't you have parents?" My eyes misted up at the thought of those words.

I shared with Zhimin a secret I kept to myself. Someone once made a pass at me in the street. It was summer time, I was wandering on a street near the hospital and was stopped by a total stranger, a sexy looking young girl many years my senior wearing tight clothes.

"Hey, kid, are you lost?"

"Go away, I don't know you."

"Well, love at the first sight. How about it, are you ready to play?"

"I don't have time!" I flatly refused her. As I was about to turn and walk away, the girl suddenly snapped me, holding my face with her two hands, and smacked me with a loud kiss.

"Her lipstick imprinted on my cheek. It smelled sweet and was bright red. Here, right in the middle of my cheek ... One

Bamboo and Little Black Skin were so envious of me." With pride, I pointed out the spot to Zhimin.

Zhimin giggled.

"Don't you believe me?"

"I do."

"Then why did you giggle?"

"She asked if you are ready to play, what did she mean by that?"

"You are a numbskull. By play, she meant to sleep with her. You see that stuff on TV all the time. I refused her because she was a tramp. You will get AIDS by sleeping with a girl like that."

This time, Zhimin giggled even harder.

I didn't tell Zhimin that One Bamboo later bought a rubber stamp with lips carved on it and used it on his own face—a ridiculous attempt on his part to impress me—out of concern that Zhimin might doubt the veracity of my story as a result.

Zhimin also shared her story with me. Zhimin confessed that she thought Shanghai was a place with skyscrapers and houses with gardens everywhere. She didn't expect that our house would not be as spacious as her own and she hadn't expected the alleyway to be so messy and dirty. Zhimin said she lied in her letters to her classmates, bragging that she lived in a high-rise.

"However, People's Square, the Bund, and Nanjing and Huaihai roads are truly beautiful. The fresh flower pavilions at the Plaza are just as pretty as foreign scenes on TV. The people in Shanghai are wealthier than those in Hefei. They have different lifestyles, they eat well, dress well, but their living conditions are not as good."

"Our area will soon be demolished. Dad said that by then our new house will be furnished like starred hotels, even better than the house of Huazi." All of a sudden I have this sense of urgency about the rumored demolition.

"Our folks in Hefei don't have the means to furnish our houses like five star hotels. You see, my classmates in Hefei called me Shanghainese a long time ago. Since I have a mother who was an educated youth from Shanghai, they naturally cast me in a different light."

"You are Shanghainese since your mom is one." I tried to please Zhimin, although I didn't regard Aunt Meizi as a Shanghai native.

"My mom has no sense of fashion. She got all of her clothes at street stands. Even I regard them as so beneath me. My mom is very good at karaoke though. In a karaoke competition organized by the factory union, she won over everyone the moment she opened her mouth. At the time, I also shared some of her glory. Mom said when they had worked in the field, singing was their only pastime and that they even learned the bel canto style singing."

"Singing is nothing to brag about. Dad said that during the days when they preached the uselessness of studying, he and his peers spent their days practicing boxing, lifting barbells, and exercising on rings. With all the specialties they mastered, they could have staged an alleyway martial art competition. They had a great time when they were young, better than ours."

"You are right. Our lives are not as exciting." Zhimin raised her head, looking nonchalant. We were standing by the ruins of the Triangle Market at the time, sunshine magically brightened this paradise of my past.

We all regretted that we missed the golden era.

Dad and the femme fatale lived in the attic after moving back. There was no need for formalities or flattering between the femme fatale and I. We were more like old acquaintances since we met a long time ago while sitting at the same table in a restaurant. We were on good terms then and kept it that way as members of the same family now. We simply went on with our lives. I later learned that Grandma and Huazi had both met the femme fatale. I had no idea what was the occasion or when they actually had sat together, nor did I know if it was deliberately arranged by Dad or a mere coincidence. The adult world seemed so mysterious to me.

Not long after Dad moved back, he did nothing, but stay at home because his business was not doing well and more than a hundred thousand yuan of his capital got stuck. Hence the femme fatale found a job somewhere else, as a female assistant at a nightclub. She was dragged back by Dad on her first day of work.

"You just stay home, do household chores, play mahjong, or watch TV. Behave yourself and don't go anywhere!" Dad ordered the femme fatale.

Grandma said Dad worried that the femme fatale might leave him for another man. Grandma added that Mom also left Dad for her boss. I insisted that it was Dad who didn't want Mom anymore.

"Don't you confuse right and wrong!" I warned Grandma.

"This is strange, you accused me of confusing right and wrong. Are you siding with your Mom or Dad?" Perplexed, Grandma looked at me and called me an idiot again.

Batting my eyes, I said nothing. I really didn't understand myself.

The femme fatale with nothing to do became a yenta, a rather pathological one, prying into the past of Mom and Dad from Grandma as if she was obsessed. This fit perfectly with Grandma's personality. She loved nothing more than dwelling on the past. The two women, one old and one young, would sit in the back alleyway whispering in private. They got along with each other just fine.

"Stinky Bug looked the most attractive in his teens. With a beautiful body and a handsome face, he was followed everywhere by hordes of crazy girls in the alleyway. The bitch came in late, but it was love at the first sight. Don't you think that Stinky Bug has an uncanny resemblance to the famous Hong Kong singer, Andy Lau?"

"No way! By the time I came along, Stinky Bug was more like an old turtle Hell, he was a bit overweight, too." The femme fatale stood up, walked a few steps and patted at Dad's behind. Wearing a cashmere sweater in a classic print and Jeanwest casual pants, Dad looked quite dashing. With his behind sticking out, he was washing vegetables by the sink. Dad always did well when he put his mind to something.

The femme fatale was also eager to find out the inside story of how Mom and Dad got married.

"This woman wouldn't let Stinky Bug out of her sight and Stinky Bug was disappointing as well … He got her pregnant. Then he had no choice, but to marry her. At the time, I pretended not to know," Grandma laughed. By the time we were eating, the femme fatale helped Grandma with a piece of fish.

"Mom, stop talking nonsense!" Dad said. Then he turned to the femme fatale, "Hell, overwhelmed by your flattery, Mom is ready to tell you anything …" Dad had a glass of beer, his face was a little flushed.

Dad asked me to get two more beers and one Sprite from Asi's store. The Sprite was meant for Zhimin and me. I ran out the door, got the stuff, and immediately ran back home. I could smell the aroma of the broth from our kitchen many doors away. Mixed with the cool air outside, I found myself thoroughly enchanted. Brimming with happiness, I could feel the liveliness and vitality of our home. All of a sudden the outside world seemed to have lost its mystique and temptation. My home filled with a kitchen aroma, much like a lighted window display at night, was drawing me in closer for more.

I no longer played outside day and night and stayed home most of the time after school. It was a time Dad needed me most as a street runner because he was renovating the kitchen himself and often needed hardware. Knowing all the stores nearby like the palm of my hand, I knew exactly where to find them.

It was a renovation on a grand scale. Dad made kitchen wall units, installed a gas-powered hot water shower, and replaced the iron gas stove that had been used for over half a century with a stainless steel one. The new shiny stove immediately brightened up the kitchen. While Dad was busy with his project, I was his indispensable assistant. Time and time again, I went out on my bicycle to buy nails, waterspout, pipes, and other things. Once amidst a roaring thunderstorm while Dad wasn't sure if I should go out, I hopped on my bike and disappeared from his sight in no time. As I quickly shuttled in and out of the narrow alleyway on my old bike, people in the alleyway all remarked, "Street Runner is mending his ways now. He is home all the time."

Like Dad, the femme fatale also liked to have me do errands for her and I was more than willing to comply. Grandma was the only family member whom I pretended not to hear. I realized later that I always shortchanged the ones I loved in life.

That was the period of time when we lived most like a family. During the day, Dad and the femme fatale usually played mahjong at home. Then they took turns to play so that one of them could cook. Three meals a day was the norm. Sometimes they would stay in the attic and watch a VCD. All the VCDs were provided by Shellac. Shellac became a collector of VCDs overnight after seeing a collection of over one thousand VCDs at his friend's place. Shellac was determined to have his own collection and Dad became the one who benefited the most from it. When Zhimin went upstairs for Beibei, I would watch the VCDs with them. I stayed away from the x-rated ones they watched. I knew the term "dirty" at the age of two and I kept my distance from pornography. What I liked were the Hollywood films—police dramas and adventure films as well as science fiction whose spectacular explosive scenes thrilled me no end.

But the good times didn't last. Grandma's condition was getting increasingly worse. She started vomiting and couldn't eat. It was summer time, Grandma was lying in bed, she no longer had the energy to get up and use the squat toilet. A small chair and a spittoon were combined to serve as a patched-up commode at her bedside. When she struggled to use the commode, the femme fatale would lend a hand. Whenever the femme fatale helped her out, Grandma would respond with a gentle smile.

Sometimes Dad and the femme fatale would go out, Grandma

would then spend all day in bed alone. She no longer watched TV and spent a lot of time sleeping, only opening her eyes every so often. Zhimin was not around either, she had registered to attend an English class in the evening. I stayed at Grandma's bedside obediently, although I was in deep fear.

"When Black Bug is not making trouble, it is not a good sign. It shows that my days are numbered. Kids have premonitions of such things." Grandma said this when the grandma of Jiajia, the one with the nickname Laolao, came to see her and praised me for staying around. Grandma was probably nostalgic for the days when I played outside with no sense of time and she dragged her feet chasing me around the alleyway. Maybe that was the time she was happy.

The strange thing is that Grandma stopped calling me Street Runner from that day on. She would only call me Black Bug. She apparently remembered that nickname of mine the most.

"I say, Black Bug, any time you should see me lying there motionless as if dead, make sure you shout at me to get my attention, or your Grandma will surely be gone." Grandma requested this of me seriously. It was evening time, Dad and the femme fatale were out. There was nothing on the dining table, and only the air conditioner was humming. The AC was bought with money pooled by Huazi, Jianguo, and Uncle. As far as money was concerned, Huazi and the others had been generous.

Grandma had a phone call with Uncle, I was the one who dialed for her. We only reached him after many transfers. In a weak voice, Grandma told Uncle, "It's time for me to bid you goodbye."

"Mom, you are too pessimistic. Huazi said that you refused to move about, life is maintained by exercise, you need to exercise."

"It's time for me to bid you goodbye." Grandma repeated her words and hung up. She turned to me and said, "This is all a show."

Even later, Grandma refused to get up and wash, and had this terrible smell about her. The femme fatale, Zhimin, and me, we all covered our noses and complained. I could tell that in daily life the femme fatale got along fine with Grandma, but she became helpless when it came to negotiating Grandma's smell. This was understandable since I also found the odor nauseating. I really pitied Grandma.

Then Dad found temporary help from an old lady from the back alleyway. She would come regularly to change Grandma's clothes and wipe her body clean. Huazi came to see Grandma and generously left a pile of money for Dad, ostensibly for buying nutritious food for Grandma and paying the domestic help.

"Mom, you have to eat. Mom, you have to move." Huazi left in a hurry. She seemed busier than ever. We later learned that Huazi was busy applying for a passport for a trip abroad.

"Grandma entertains no illusion now. This is all a show." Seeing the money left behind by Huazi, Grandma told me once again. I wasn't sure that I understood her.

During that time, Dad took Grandma to see a doctor by taxi. In the habit of doing things right, Dad registered to see a specialist and that took them a good half-day of waiting in the hot summer weather. During the appointment, Dad pleaded with the doctor to have Grandma admitted to the hospital. He didn't expect this retort from the doctor, "Is this hospital yours?" The doctor also told us coldly that we were at the wrong place and that we should have seen someone at the outpatient department. And the office hours for the outpatient department had just come to an end.

"Go, let's go home!" Broken-hearted, Grandma ordered Dad. This was the last show of Grandma's strong personality. Dad could only sheepishly follow the order and carried Grandma on his back home.

Later, Dad called Huazi for help. Huazi said, "Why do you always ask for my help? I am not omnipotent. If you have a problem, go to the hospital. If the doctor says you are ok, you are ok. I am not a doctor."

"Hell, Mom is sick. Who else to ask for help but you? A nonfamily member?" When Dad raised his voice rudely, Huazi cut him off by hanging up.

"Tell Huazi, it's time for me to settle the score with her. She has always been the most finicky one since childhood. I never asked her to do any household chores with her delicate hands. During the Cultural Revolution, between her and Meizi, one of them had to go to the countryside. Huazi being the dainty kind, I couldn't bear the thought of her doing hard labor. I had a secret talk with the teacher of Meizi and arranged to have Meizi go instead of her sister. I let Meizi down ..." In a feeble voice, Grandma slowly let out the story and started crying.

"Mom, this is something totally new to me. Does Meizi know?"

"She doesn't, but Huazi knows. That is why she came out in support of Zhimin's return. In fact, even if Huazi kept quiet on the matter, I still wanted to help out Zhimin. Once her household registration is back in Shanghai, I will die a happy person." Sobbing, Grandma used the back of her hand to wipe away the smears of tears and mucus.

Zhimin stood there stunned. The other day, Grandma again trashed Meizi, saying that she was hiding in Hefei having a good time. Zhimin argued with Grandma and had not spoken to her for three days. Now, her eyes were red, not uttering a word. I realized only then that Meizi was the one Grandma worried about the most. This revelation baffled me. Grandma cared for Meizi the most, but she scolded her the most and kept her at a distance. Little did I know that I shared this same personality trait with Grandma.

Six months after Mom left the family, she called me one day out of the blue. She asked me to join her right away at a hot pot restaurant called "Family Reunion" on Jiujiang Road where someone was giving a party. I'd been to that restaurant with Dad and I knew that it was a buffet restaurant where you could choose BBQ, hot pot, or western dishes. They also served all kinds of desserts and drinks. You could pick and choose what to eat and eat as much as you wanted. But I tersely said no. Mom pleaded with me over the phone while Dad and the femme fatale coldly stared at me. I swallowed my saliva.

"I am not going!" I refused Mom and hung up the phone. I returned to my homework without saying a word to Dad or the femme fatale. I realized that I was quite good at putting on a show.

I missed my mom and I wept in silence that night. It was then that I finally came to understand my personality.

Grandma was finally hospitalized. She was sometimes lucid, sometimes confused, and was unable to take care of herself. Huazi hired a high-priced nursing assistant Auntie Wu for Grandma after consulting Jianguo and Dad. She went to the hospital daily, always in a hurry. Wearing elegant professional suits and an exquisite handbag, Huazi especially stood out in the hospital environment. Grandma told Auntie Wu that Huazi was a busy person.

"Old lady, you are so lucky to have such an outstanding daughter," Auntie Wu commented flatteringly.

Huazi used her cell phone to call long distance to Meizi as well as the Uncle in Beijing, informing them of Grandma's condition, "Mom's hospital expenses plus the cost of having a nursing assistant at least will amount to five or six thousand yuan. We should all contribute one thousand each, and you will be informed of the situation as appropriate." Huazi was clear-headed and her remarks were short and to the point, a testimony of her being a capable person.

I heard that Meizi was startled by that phone call. In a tone expressing some difficulties, she said that she would mail in the money the next day.

The next day, Meizi called Huazi. "Huazi, you are the elder sister and you have always helped me. Is it possible for you to go easy on me with money? I can't come up with a thousand yuan on short notice. This is what I think. You have hired a nursing assistant, right? A nursing assistant is expensive and not as caring. I will take a leave to care for Mom, and then we can all save money. To tell you the truth, even if money wasn't an issue I would still want to care for Mom myself."

"I can empathize with you. But this is not something that I can make the decision all by myself. Moreover, every time you are here, you two always fight. I need to ask Mom before anything is finalized."

I heard that upon learning that Meizi might come, Grandma's eyes suddenly brightened up. "Of course, I want her. I want my own child. Where is she?" When asked by Huazi, Grandma became anxious. In a somewhat confused state, Grandma looked around everywhere, thinking that Meizi was already there.

"Fine, I will inform Meizi right away. She should be here by tomorrow. Mom, promise me you won't fight this time."

"I won't. I will not fight her." Grandma nodded readily. Grandma in sickness was as meek as a child.

From that moment on, Grandma had been looking forward to Meizi's arrival. She kept on repeating, "Tomorrow, tomorrow …"

I accompanied Meizi to the hospital after her arrival to Shanghai. The hospital was where I played since childhood. I had witnessed with my own eyes the horror of childbirth. No other place was as familiar to me as this hospital.

The meeting of Meizi and Grandma was heartbreaking. They embraced and cried their eyes out. The small frame of Meizi snuggled next to Grandma's, heaved in constant sobs.

"Mommy, I am here, and I will take care of you until you can leave the hospital fully recovered …" Meizi repeated in tears these consoling words. Like Huazi, she would change the way she addressed Grandma, from Mom to Mommy at certain times—an intimate term they used while they were young.

"Meizi, everything is fine now that you are here. I want to tell you that Zhimin is a good child. Make sure you take care of her and not let her repeat what you went through." Grandma's eyebrows were tightly knit together while uttering these words. By then she was already incontinent and also obviously in great pain.

Meizi choked in sobs. She never left the hospital after this. For three months, one hundred days in total and twenty-four hours a day, Meizi was taking good care of Grandma. Sleeping with her clothes on and with constant interruptions, Meizi stayed until Grandma passed away

Afterwards, she was sick for a long time. While in bed recovering, Meizi would become emotional and tears would roll down her eyes every time the subject of Grandma came up. Meizi was an emotionally weak woman who gave into tears easily.

One day at the hospital, I was suddenly hit by an idea. Without really knowing what was to come, I cajoled Auntie Wu into accompanying me to see dead bodies at the morgue. I peered inside at the door of the unassuming room. All I saw was a tightly closed giant iron cabinet with rust all over. Auntie Wu said, "This is the icebox where the bodies are stored." I thought Auntie Wu was merely trying to scare me, since I didn't believe that after death people would "sleep" in such a crummy place. As I tried to decipher the mystery, three people were approaching us pushing a small bed with wheels. A long package wrapped in blue cloth lay on the bed.

"The dead body is coming," Auntie Wu uttered with a soft scream. After this, she covered her mouth and fled the scene.

The old man pushing the cart opened one of the iron drawers in the morgue, and an icy cold long iron case came into view. I immediately realized that this was indeed the place where the dead "slept." When the two family members moved the blue package into the case as directed by the old man, they didn't look sad, but cold and distant.

"Our dad had suffered enough, it's finally over." One of the members remarked to the old man while putting down his signature. With a strange smile on his face, the old man didn't respond in words. He had apparently seen way too many deaths.

Was it a coincidence that in this hospital I witnessed both the bloodiness of childbirth and the cruelty of death? I now understood that for life and death, their ordinary pain and heroism would always coexist in contrast of each other. When the pain stopped, so would life.

I found out about Grandma's passing during noon recess. Meizi called from the hospital. Sobbing, she said, "They were trying to revive her at first ..." But before she could finish her sentence, all Meizi could say, "She is gone, Mom is gone." The line was then cut off. Dad and the femme fatale rushed to the hospital right away. After they left, I had the sense to spread the news to the uncle in Beijing, Jianguo, and Huazi.

Huazi was abroad. It was her colleague who answered the phone.

"Grandma is gone." I repeated the same message to Jianguo.

"Who said that? Don't you cry wolf like Grandma. Where is your Dad?" Jianguo didn't believe when I told him.

"Grandma is gone," I murmured.

At that juncture, the clock of the St. Francis tower suddenly rang out. Perhaps it was some kind of response from the big clock that Grandma trusted the most in life. The sound of the clock seemed to have struck a chord in my heart. Tears rolled down my cheeks in spite of myself.

I finally realized that Grandma was actually the one person that I loved the most. But lying in a cold iron case, she could no longer chase me, scold me, or beep Dad to give me a round of beating. In retrospect, all I could find in those past events was Grandma's love.

A long time afterwards, Dad was about to go on a business trip one morning and was having a puff sitting in the back alleyway before leaving. He rubbed his eyes overwhelmed by a sudden sense of sorrow.

"Gee, what happened?" the femme fatale asked him.

"Nothing, I just remembered Mom. If she were alive, she would always go on and on with her kind advice knowing that I was about to go on a trip."

"Well, I will be the one to do that now. Haven't I been

reminding you of things?"

"It's different. You advised me not to sleep around, whereas Mom's concerns were about if I had enough clothes and money for the road. In her own words, practice thrift at home, but be amply provided for while traveling."

"Hell, you don't think my advice is good?" The femme fatale tittered as she put newly made liquor preserved crabs in the refrigerator. She was a capable proprietress by now. Dad opened a small restaurant at home. His great cooking skills were finally put to use.

That morning after having breakfast at our home restaurant, I waved goodbye to Dad and the femme fatale. But I didn't go to school, I went to the funeral home where Grandma's ashes were stored. Last night, I dreamt of Grandma sitting in the back alleyway. She complained, "Why won't you let me wear socks, it is freezing cold here." Getting up in the morning, I found that the weather was really cold. I bought a pair of terrycloth socks for Grandma at a nearby store and left them by her urn. I hoped Grandma would like them. Afterwards, I thought about the things that I'd like to tell her. I am now in junior high. Also, the junior school I go to has a clock tower, the clock has been clicking for more than a hundred years and will continue for another one hundred or even two hundred years more ... One thing I wasn't sure if I should tell Grandma was that Mom and I had met once in secret. Mom had obviously stopped dyeing her hair for some time since black hair could be seen near her scalp. Her lipstick was not done properly either. I guess, she wasn't having an easy time. She went on and on about how she hated Dad. The fact that she cared so much about Dad may have been a sign that she still loved him. The mere thought of it saddened me.

Later I dreamt of swimming in the river in front of our house. There was a lot of garbage and dead rats in the water, much like the Suzhou River. How could there be a river under the eaves? I never even asked myself that obvious question. I only know that by the time I climbed to the riverbanks, I had already grown up.

Jiqing Li

The taxi driver refused to go inside the alleyway because it was too narrow for cars. The driver explained to Xiaoyu that he would only make an exception for a bride on her wedding day, an unwritten rule for all taxis. Renyan then boldly challenged the driver, "How do you know she is not a bride?" And he, by implication, the bridegroom. A somewhat embarrassed Xiaoyu quickly shut him down and stepped out of the car.

Xiaoyu was moving into a place in one of Shanghai's alleyways. Her boyfriend Renyan was helping out, carrying her belongings without any complaints. Xiaoyu grew up in modern apartment complexes in Shanghai, a lovely girl with delicate features and a sunny outlook. But surprisingly to Xiaoyu, people she met on assignments outside the city would always say that she didn't look like a typical Shanghainese.

"You're Shanghainese?" This was usually a question her friends from other cities would ask early on. They couldn't pinpoint what was missing, but they all concluded with an air of certainty that Xiaoyu didn't look like a young lady from Shanghai. They might have meant it as a compliment. After all, the Shanghainese image wasn't that great in the rest of China, but Xiaoyu had a strong attachment to her hometown. She couldn't help but envy the girls who grew up in alleyways—they seemed smart and meticulous, gentle and proud, and carried themselves with confidence. Was it because they embodied the elegance of the Bund and the culture of the city residents? In the summer when she saw those beautiful girls coming out of the alleyway, she would think they were the most alluring city dwellers.

Quite unexpectedly, her dream of being one of these girl

from the alleyway finally came true. The wife of a colleague of hers, an extremely resourceful woman, managed to pry a room from her work unit in the alleyway for herself at no cost and wanted to rent it out. Xiaoyu, the first to get the news, jumped at this opportunity and got it cheap for 300 yuan a month.

"They say that this place will never be up for demolition. It is bound to be the last alleyway of Shanghai of this century," Renyan said. He raised his head and noted the three big characters "Jiqing Li" (Auspicious Alleyway) as well as the other lucky patterns engraved on the stone gate guarding the alleyway entrance.

"In that case, I will be a witness to history then," Xiaoyu said. Then she looked up at the stone gate and noted the year "1897" written on it. If true, Jiqing Li was more than a hundred years old by now. She wondered how many spirits wandered in and out of the alleyway and the vicissitudes they had witnessed through the years.

"This is the Bronx of Shanghai, you still have time to change your mind," Renyan said this as he stared down the deep and narrow alleyway. Bamboo poles one after another filled the narrow sky of the alleyway, on them hung colorful washed clothes, including dripping, wrinkly wet diapers that looked fatigued.

"This is the place that I've been wanting for so long. I'll finally be the girl from the alleyway now. However undesirable it may be, it is better than what you have. Still living with your parents in the same apartment, you should be ashamed," Xiaoyu complained to Renyan and breathed in an air of excitement. After seeing the year 1897 carved on the stone gate, she started fantasizing about the Jiqing Li and its past.

"What's so special about the girls from the alleyway? They treat the alleyway as their living room, walking about in pajamas with their hair unkept and seem to giggle for no good reason. They love to gather in groups to chat about nothing important while spreading rumors," Renyan retorted.

"You grew up in the alleyway yourself, are you dismissing it simply because you have moved on to a new building? If you can't keep your mouth shut, I will not let you help me move anymore," said Xiaoyu as she shoved Renyan aside.

"All kinds of people reside in alleyways, con men, female drug addicts and so on. Just be careful. You might come to regret your decision one day." Renyan grumbled after he said this and followed her lead.

Renyan lived in a three-bedroom apartment in a new development in Meilong District. As his parents' only child, he and his parents were hoping that Xiaoyu would agree to move in with them, as his former girlfriend did for two long years. After they broke up, he had several other girlfriends, but none of them worked out until he met Xiaoyu. But Xiaoyu guarded her last line of defense really hard, and now she even decided to move into an old style stone gate building by herself. How could he stop from complaining?

"How come you are an even bigger nag than my mother? Actually, what worries my mother the most is you. She is afraid that you only have sexual intentions and will take advantage of me," Xiaoyu said this as she impatiently turned around to Renyan.

"Wouldn't it be nice if I indeed had the means of taking advantage of you and making you my de facto bride," Renyan said. He found her remarks both funny and annoying.

"Like a fox guarding the henhouse, you do have ulterior motives. Well, you might as well dream on, no wedding, no way." Xiaoyu smiled and turned around, putting her arms around Renyan. This was typical of the mannerisms of Shanghai girls, they are gentle and insistent, while leaving their boys feeling helpless and needed at the same time.

"Be careful of my fantasies though," Renyan said with a trace of lust.

"Are you proposing? Unfortunately, you are too young. The most fashionable men today are those middle-aged successful ones. So you have to wait patiently for your turn." Xiaoyu coquettishly rubbed his nose with her finger.

A crowd in front of one of the households in the alleyway then caught their attention, it sounded like a fight was going on. Xiaoyu squeezed her way in for a closer look. Renyan stayed in the back. He had no interest in these quarrels of minor importance.

A short man was shouting at the man standing at the gate. "You son of a bitch, how dare you asking me to sign a PM contract like that? My wife died already. What do you think I even care about anymore? Nothing is holding me back now. I am ready to commit murder, arson or do anything that may shock the city of Shanghai if push comes to shove."

And the man at the gate, which appeared to be his former boss was younger-looking and with a sore on his mouth. He showed no signs of retreat and retorted even more fiercely, gesticulating with his fists.

"I am not afraid of anything. Why don't you come now and have it out with me! Come on! Unlike managers of profit-making plants, I don't have bodyguards or life insurance, and I have nothing to lose! Do you think I want to be the lousy plant manager? Look at the place I live, a mere 15 square-meter area. Even my wife looks down upon me. What kind of a bullshit manager I am! The banks and the court are after me for debt repayment. I worried so much and this open sore can serve as my witness. Who would be willing to take over the plant and who can I go to for help?" The plant manager unbuttoned his shirt, as if he was prepared for whatever was in store for him. The short man was at a loss of what to do next.

"You are the vicious Emperor Qin, you are a fascist! Whoever you are, I am determined to stay put at your place. If I go home, I'll have nothing to eat anyway, my daughter needs to go to school …" The short man started to cry at these words.

"What's the use of going after the plant manager, he's all by himself," said someone in the crowd. "You are still an able-bodied man, why don't you go to the labor market and see if there are opportunities. If not, you can still sell box lunches or do hourly work, there must be a way out."

The plant manager began to speak to the crowd once he realized that some of them were on his side. "The plant has no money, not even one cent, only the piece of land it sits on. It's a state asset and I have nothing to do with it. Even the telephone company threatened to cut our line. I have been following closely the labor market news every day, and have been to all places I can think of to beg for help. I worked so hard that the soles of my shoes are torn. What else can I do? Whenever an opening comes up, whom should I give it to among the hundreds of applicants? He stands a better chance of finding something if he spends his time at the labor market and not here."

Xiaoyu listened when a middle-aged woman began explaining PM contracts in detail. It is a "retention of labor relations agreement" signed between the unemployed and the work unit. The work unit agrees to continue to provide a pension and medical insurance for the departed worker for the period as specified in the agreement. In return, the worker agrees not to get unemployment subsidy from the work unit and to be on his or her own. To put it bluntly, a PM contract was a pink slip.

The woman continued, "I also signed a PM contract. Find employment? It's not easy at all! I still have four more years to go before the age of retirement. I am dealing with it one day at a time, others eat meat and I eat preserved vegetables. Fortunately, my kid is now working." The woman seemed to have been deeply touched by the plight of her fellow workers, she stayed a while longer and left before the drama ended.

"You see how chaotic lives in the alleyway are. In the days when I grew up in the alleyway housewives were everywhere, and when they fought, their rude postures and colorful abusive language were second to none," Renyan said. He came to take Xiaoyu away from the crowd and continued to criticize alleyway lives.

"I hope we will not become useless in society when we are middle-aged. Have you seen the movie *Network Existence*? In the future, the way of human existence will undergo changes." Without responding to his comment, Xiaoyu followed Renyan and left the crowd.

Xiaoyu's new place was a garret apartment at Number 12. A garret was considered a rather undesirable living space in the alleyway, known for its cramped quarters and poor exposure because it faced the north and west. It is wedged between the first and the second floor, underneath it is the shared kitchen. In the evening during the summer, the garret becomes insufferable by the heat from the kitchen underneath and the burning sun that shines in from the west window.

"In the days before air conditioning, it was pretty hard to live in the garret," said Renyan while pointing at the window AC. The apartment looked sparse with its old-styled armoire, a simple table, and several chairs.

"The furniture was all lent to me by my colleagues. Do you know that Shanghai garrets are quite famous? Many well-known writers stayed in garrets during their difficult years. Haven't you heard that garrets were cradles for writers? But I don't want to be a writer, they tend to be hypocrites nowadays." Xiaoyu opened up her luggage and put things in the armoire.

"I think you are a writer, but instead of throwing words around, you are a Shanghai young lady throwing temper tantrums."

"Is that what you really think? You don't know how lucky you are that you haven't run into a real Shanghai young lady with overdramatic temper tantrums!" Xiaoyu pointed her finger at the forehead of Renyan.

"Ok, I am lucky, really lucky! I will bring my computer with me the next time and leave it here, so that we have something to play with later." Renyan nodded repeatedly and apologetically in response to Xiaoyu's stare. During his college years, he had been known for turning dorm rooms into computer game rooms.

"Don't you ever think that you can turn my room into a game room!" Xiaoyu warned Renyan with a fierce look.

"I will teach you how to log on the Internet," Renyan immediately offered. Then in an effort to demonstrate his good will, he tried to hold Xiaoyu for a kiss.

Xiaoyu broke herself away from Renyan once she heard someone say "Miss" at the door. Poking her head inside was Mother Zhang who lived in the front part (the second floor) of the building whom she met before when she came to look at this place. And "Miss" was the way she had addressed Xiaoyu from the very beginning. "Miss, have you moved in? No wonder the spider in my room had spun a web, we now have a new neighbor. I am on my way down to cook. My son owns a restaurant and these are the condiments that he gave me. Do you need any help? And this is …" Mother Zhang was politely eying Renyan while holding her basket filled with bottles and containers of various sizes.

"Oh, he is my friend, he is here to lend me a hand," Xiaoyu hastily said

"Yes, yes, a young man, of course," Mother Zhang responded rather awkwardly with a knowing smile on her face as she turned around and went downstairs. Xiaoyu knew what that smile really meant. Mother Zhang probably thought she was too easy around men.

"You see, this is the life of the alleyway, there is no privacy. Besides, the older women here are especially shrewd, they can see through anything. Just close the door," Renyan complained to Xiaoyu.

"I won't. People will think that we are doing something inappropriate. Why can't you behave and keep your hands to yourself? Look at the way you are, it's no wonder that my mother doesn't trust you." As she uttered these words, she took the initiative of holding Renyan's face in her hand and kissed him.

"Why, who is misbehaving now? Women are indeed fickle creatures." Renyan dodged his face away from Xiaoyu's.

"You are not to talk about women! So I misbehaved. Don't you like it?" Xiaoyu simply hated the word "women." She felt that it was a term for the married ones or for ladies who are at least in their thirties.

"As the saying goes, if a man is chasing after a woman, he has to break a wall. If a woman is after a man, she only has to break a paper barrier. Of course, I want you to put the moves on me, the more the better. Come on." Renyan decided to do away with all pretenses and shamelessly put his face next to Xiaoyu's.

"You're thick skinned!" Xiaoyu found it so hilarious.

While they were laughing and kissing, Xiaoyu turned around and found that someone was watching them from across the street. They had stopped kissing, but she couldn't help from bursting out in laugher again.

"Hey, tell me, Mother Zhang went downstairs to cook, why was she carrying all those bottles and containers?" Xiaoyu asked.

"The kitchen is a shared space. Mother Zhang must have decided to carry all her condiments and spices in and out so that no one can use or steal them. She guards her things as treasures and doesn't mind the hassle of carrying them. This is how people behave in the alleyway. You should watch out in your contact with the others as well," Renyan reminded Xiaoyu.

"Have you called our son? Your birthday is coming next month, is he going to do anything about it? Maybe send a token gift of one or two thousand yuan?" From the kitchen underneath an old man was saying, perhaps half-jokingly. Xiaoyu learned later that the voice belonged to the husband of Mother Zhang.

"Why, you are so obsessed with money! Reminding him of my birthday for some money? Nowadays, grandchildren are being taken care of by their grandparents and sons are no longer paying respect to their parents." Mother Zhang's voice was heard in response.

"That's absurd! I will move in with him tomorrow and see if he dares not to serve me meals in respect!" He raised his voice as if in anger.

"Enough! You are full of hot air and no action. You are the one who spoiled our son. On your seventieth birthday next year,

I will ask them for a gift. As for my birthday, just let it go." After Mother Zhang's compromise proposal, the old man's grumble finally died down.

"You can hear real human drama every day now. And for free." Seeing that Xiaoyu was listening so attentively to the conversation downstairs, he purposefully walked over and opened the door even wider.

"You!" Annoyed, Xiaoyu gave Renyan a shove. Renyan stumbled and fell on Xiaoyu's kettle. The kettle rested on its side and all of its water spilled over the floor.

"Miss, what's happening in your apartment? There's water dripping down on my washed vegetables." Mother Zhang was screaming downstairs, sounding flustered. Renyan and Xiaoyu were looking at each other not knowing how to respond. Xiaoyu finally screamed back, "Sorry, my kettle fell over. I'll be more careful in the future!"

Xiaoyu then washed her hair and sat across Renyan.

"My dear, I just love the way you look after you washed your hair." Renyan was staring tenderly at Xiaoyu. Having lived with his former girlfriend for two years, Renyan exuded a natural maturity. It was probably this quality that Xiaoyu found so attractive.

At this moment, a mosquito flew in, buzzing back and forth between Xiaoyu and Renyan. Xiaoyu asked Renyan to end the life of this unwanted guest.

"Only old houses will have mosquitoes these days," Renyan grumbled. After many tries and a lot of misses, he finally succeeded in killing the hateful creature.

Xiaoyu remembered the first time they met. Not given a chance to protest, she was dragged by Little Monkey, her college classmate, to a teahouse close to her apartment in her slippers and with freshly washed hair falling about her. At the time, a middle-aged married man whom Xiaoyu met through her boss Lenny at a party was trying hard to ingratiate himself with her. Lenny was a female engineer from Germany. The man was checking the authenticity of a blue vase—a piece claimed to be of the era of Emperor Qianlong of the Qing Dynasty—that Lenny bought. As expected, the vase turned out to be a fake. This middle-aged man worked hard, was quite established in his profession and was also a man with good taste. He often asked Xiaoyu and Lenny to go to the antique market along Dongtai Road with him. Gradually, Xiaoyu learned to appreciate and love the old stuff of Shanghai.

The carved makeup case cherished by Xiaoyu was bought at Dongtai Road. Looking at herself in the antique mirror from the early republican days, Xiaoyu would become obsessed with a lingering emotion of the past every time. Xiaoyu was ambivalent about dating because of this man. She liked how he seemed to enjoy life and the city. She wasn't that interested in dating, even feeling uneasy about it. She worried that she would be disappointed at young men of her own age.

Little Monkey didn't know what was on Xiaoyu's mind. Little Monkey was a girl with a big heart, and eager to play matchmaker for those she thought would make good couples. She once told Xiaoyu half-jokingly that she intended to send a hundred couples to the altar and she herself would be in the last pair. This time, she intended to introduce Xiaoyu to a colleague of hers who worked in the planning office, a graduate from the highly regarded Tongji University. He reportedly was quite accomplished in his profession and was well liked by the opposite sex.

"Truth be told, I find him a good catch, too. I have been thinking of saving him for myself someday. Let's just say that you agree to be his temporary girlfriend. Then as he matures, he may become more likable to the ladies." Little Monkey let go of her fancy rather shamelessly.

"So you want to enjoy other people's hard labor? How do you know you will not be the one to lose everything?" When Xiaoyu was dragged into the teahouse, she thought to herself, she would agree to be "friends" with this man if he also had a head of wet hair. It so happened that Renyan just had his hair washed and was sitting casually at a seat by the window. Seeing Little Monkey and Xiaoyu, he broke into an unpretentious smile. Xiaoyu immediately felt her heartbeat quickened, as if it was meant to be.

Renyan told Xiaoyu afterwards that when he sat in the teahouse waiting, he hadn't really given much thought to the meeting. He didn't expect Little Monkey to bring over an extraordinary beauty, he was merely there to kill time. But when he caught sight of Xiaoyu in her slippers, her wet hair falling wherever they may be, he realized that Xiaoyu cared even less about the meeting than he did. Suddenly, all his laid-back senses came back to life.

That was how love between Xiaoyu and Renyan started unexpectedly. After becoming friends, they realized that they had so much in common. For instance, they were reading the same book, *The Joke* by Milan Kundera; they enjoyed the same movie, *Mo' Better Blues* with Denzel Washington; they both liked the bustling and modern cities like Shanghai, their hometown, and New York City in the United States ... What interested Xiaoyu the most was to listen to Renyan's detailed explanation of the architectural style and the historical changes to the old and the new buildings that came into view as they walked on the street together. Xiaoyu was very much impressed by his extensive knowledge, the analogies he used, and his understanding of architecture.

Having Renyan around, Xiaoyu finally came out of the emotional trap set up by the middle-aged man. But Xiaoyu had learned a lot from this man, from lessons of life to how to deal with people and how to behave—some of them her parents never imparted to her—both from the way he carried himself and through his patient tutoring. Even more important to her was that Xiaoyu learned from him the pleasures of life, such as sampling tea, appreciating collections, and flirting. Xiaoyu knew from the very beginning that this man was only a diversion in her life and not her final destination. She was not a girl only after romance, she knew and understood the rules for city life.

Xiaoyu didn't mind that much about the Renyan's previous relationship with his live-in girlfriend. In fact, she would not agree to move in with Renyan no matter what. More than six months into their relationship, Xiaoyu came to accept the kisses, hugs and caresses of Renyan. These intimate contacts with the opposite sex had aroused her, but she refused to make love with Renyan, for reasons even she herself didn't really understand. Maybe she was trying to make a point to Renyan that not all girls nowadays would readily agree to a live-in arrangement, or maybe deep in her heart she still hadn't let go of the middle-aged man?

At evening time, Huang Jiajia, her neighbor on the first floor came over when Xiaoyu was doing some small washing at the tap spout downstairs. Huang Jiajia was a charming young woman with a pretty face and an attractive figure.

"How do you do? My name is Huang Jiajia, I am your downstairs neighbor." Huang Jiajia seemed lonely as she eagerly tried to strike a conversation with Xiaoyu, "Just let me know the next time you want to use the washing machine. I have a Prodigy washer which is easy to load and unload, you are welcome to use it."

"There is really no need, I can do serious laundry at my mother's." Xiaoyu nodded at her with gratitude.

"I work at a department store on Huaihai Road as a bookkeeper, how about you?" Huang Jiajia asked Xiaoyu rather directly.

"I work as a translator at a German automobile company in Shanghai," Xiaoyu replied.

"Wow, are you dealing with foreigners daily? You must be very smart. Mother Zhang, our new garret neighbor is a translator, a very smart girl." Huang Jiajia was really impressed and she even yelled the news to Mother Zhang who happened to be walking upstairs.

"She is young and grew up at the right time. As the old saying goes, timing is more important than experience. You are also doing great yourself, unlike our generation who had worked our heads off our whole life," Mother Zhang responded without a pause in her steps on the wooden stairs. She was holding something like an oil bottle in her hand. The stairs creaked at her every step. Listening to Mother Zhang speaking the dialogue particular to the alleyway and seeing her negotiating the stairs up and down so skillfully, Xiaoyu started having the feeling that her move to the alleyway was a right decision.

"The one who dropped by this morning, is he your boyfriend? He is a dapper-looking young man. Nice choice," said Huang Jiajia. Xiaoyu just smiled.

Huang Jiajia was facing the back entrance of the alleyway that closes only at nighttime. Looking at the back alleyway and with an air of mystery, she told Xiaoyu that the man sitting in the back was a pervert. His wife went to Japan for work and never came back, and he became a pervert as a result.

"You have to be careful, I've heard that he'll unexpectedly grab any woman that comes his way for a kiss," Huang Jiajia alerted Xiaoyu. Xiaoyu became nervous and tried to turn around and get a good look of the man, but Huang Jiajia waved her hand and stopped her. Xiaoyu noticed that her fingernails were painted purple, an odd choice of color.

"Don't turn around, he will get suspicious. If he chooses to charge towards us, we will be in big trouble," Huang Jiajia told her. She stayed around and chatted about something else for a while. When her house phone rang, she ran back to her room to answer it. Xiaoyu couldn't help, but to turn around and look.

It just so happened that the pervert stood up and left the moment Huang Jiajia walked away, and another man came and sat down in his place. The man was covered in sweat after doing some strenuous exercise. When Xiaoyu turned around, it was this man that came into her view. But she didn't know that. When the man saw Xiaoyu looking at him, he smiled at her. Xiaoyu panicked. She forced herself to smile back and hoped he wouldn't come her way. Little did she expect that the man nodded at her again, still wearing a smile. Xiaoyu's heartbeat quickened.

"You must be new here? So very young!" The man seemed very friendly.

Xiaoyu said to herself, Huang Jiajia was right. This guy was a pervert, just look at his bedroom eyes and his heavy sweating. My goodness, he was in heat! Then the thought of preventing him from hugging or kissing her crossed her mind. Those with a psychological problem are not held responsible for their behavior, even killing, so the best way out of the present danger was to flee the scene. As Xiaoyu was planning her escape, the man already had straightened up and started walking over. Xiaoyu ducked into Huang Jiajia's room in desperation. To her surprise, the man followed her way in as well.

"Huang Jiajia, the pervert, the pervert is here ..." Xiaoyu was so scared that she was incoherent and could hardly keep herself from crumbling down.

"Where?" Huang Jiajia asked cluelessly.

"Right after me, right here." Xiaoyu pointed at the man who followed her in, she couldn't even finish her sentence before her legs gave way and she fell to the ground. When Huang Jiajia raised her head and saw a confused looking man behind Xiaoyu, she roared in laughter.

That was how Xiaoyu unexpectedly showed up at Huang Jiajia's place the first time. She had mistaken Huang Jiajia's husband for the pervert. He had just finished practicing football with their son at a lot razed for urban renewal nearby, which had gotten him very sweaty. He knew that a white-collared young lady would be moving into the garret and approached Xiaoyu to say hello. No one could've expected that his innocent gesture would cause such a brouhaha.

Now all three of them laughed so hard until they gasped for air. Later, Huang Jiajia asked Xiaoyu to stay for a chat in their living room. She was both curious and excited at this invitation because she never stopped by her neighbors for small talks when she lived in apartment buildings. The home of Huang Jiajia had a small courtyard in the back. A wing-room was connected with the living room in the front. Huang Jiajia seemed pleased to have the opportunity to lead Xiaoyu for a quick walk-through. Being a smart girl, Xiaoyu knew that Huang Jiajia, as is typical of all Shanghai girls, would be more than pleased to get positive responses from during the house tour. Out of courtesy and genuine feeling, Xiaoyu oohed and aahed as they moved along.

It was indeed an exquisitely decorated home. Xiaoyu noticed that the living room was furnished with traditional rosewood furniture. A twin bed was tucked in at one corner, on it laid a small soft pillow with a cute cartoon design. It must be the bed of their child. The wing-room apparently served as the couples' sitting room, it was a room of about 20 square meters, spacious and formal. A bonus room was added on top of the wing-room. Sizing up the elegant European-style furniture, the stereo system, the thousands of VCDs discs, and Huang Jiajia's purple nail polish, Xiaoyu was surprised at the sight of such a wonderful mixture of the East and the West in this old building. She asked herself if this was where the alleyway culture came from.

Standing in front of the shelf filled with discs, Xiaoyu only allowed herself some quick glances, in spite of her great love for disks. One of Xiaoyu's strong points was that she would never go through other people's belongings, not even her best friend's things. It was this attention to detail that made Xiaoyu such a sympathetic and graceful girl. Huang Jiajia offered to invite her over for disc viewing someday. Xiaoyu nodded, and pointed to the boy in one of the pictures in the wing-room, "This must be your son, he's just as beautiful as you are."

Huang Jiajia smiled and said his name was Tianye, which meant a field. His father's name is Jin Ming: Jin as in gold and Ming as in bright. "We named our son with both of our surnames, so his full name is Jinhuang Tianye, the golden yellow field."

Jin Ming added, "My name has only two characters and my son has four characters. As the saying goes, the younger generation is expected to outperform the older ones."

This time it was Xiaoyu's turn to chuckle. Xiaoyu asked, "Does it mean that Tianye would need six characters for his offspring? I heard that there is a guy in Belgium with a name composed of 150 words and it takes several minutes just to read it out."

According to Huang Jiajia, when Jin Ming went to the police station to register the birth, the policeman in charge of the household registry rejected the child's name because it was too westernized. Jin Ming threatened to sue them for violation of his human rights. They finally relented after six months of haggling. Huang Jiajia said that they both were busy in their respective companies, so they left their child full-time with a well-equipped kindergarten whose fees were enormous, of course.

"So far Jin Ming can still afford it," Huang Jiajia declared without much fanfare. Xiaoyu didn't ask anymore questions about it, she knew that income is a family's most guarded secret. She wouldn't ask for the information if it was not given voluntarily. What Xiaoyu didn't know was that by being sensitive and sympathetic, she already possessed the good qualities of the alleyway girls and she had passed the test with flying colors.

"I used to be slimmer than you are now. I was known to have the devil's figure. Giving birth proved to be a curse for me, that figure is gone forever," said Huang Jiajia as she was staring at the graceful line of Xiaoyu full of envy.

"Marriage was the curse for me, because it condemned me to a life without freedom forever," Jin Ming interjected. "Get lost," Huang Jiajia said to him. "We were making girl talk, men are not allowed to chime in." Jin Ming shook his head as if in frustration while Huang Jiajia smiled again.

Xiaoyu liked Huang Jiajia's family courtyard, small with natural light. It brought in extra brightness and comfort to the cramp old building. An oleander plant was growing in there. What was most interesting was the well that appeared in the courtyard, a curious sight for Xiaoyu who grew up in the city. The floor-to-ceiling glass door that separated the living room and the courtyard also exuded classical elegance. Huang Jiajia told Xiaoyu that there was a green snake living in the courtyard, who had been spotted by people of the older generation. "It is a house snake, our guardian angel." Huang Jiajia disclosed this piece of intriguing information cryptically.

Later on when Xiaoyu was on the phone with Renyan, she talked endlessly about the small courtyard of the Huang family. Influenced by Xiaoyu, Renyan was in a nostalgic mood all of a sudden, and started reminiscing about his days in the old stone gate housing. He often wrestled with friends in his own family courtyard and got black and blue. He also remembered trying to catch the crickets in the courtyard on summer nights. "As soon as you located them to the east, they would jump to the west, and as soon as you turned towards the west, their chirping would come from the east—a good night sleep was out of the question." As he described it, the courtyard in his old stone gate housing became more like the vegetable garden of Lu Xun's (a well-known Chinese writer) childhood, a most exciting place. As he spoke, Xiaoyu's thoughts drifted to when she was chatting with Huang Jiajia earlier. Jin Ming had ducked into the wing-room to watch a football match on TV. "If it weren't for the football match, Jin Ming wouldn't stay home without protesting," Huang Jiajia told Xiaoyu. Tianye came home later. He was a sunny-looking six-year-old with a solid build. Like a gentleman, he turned towards Xiaoyu and said, "How do you do, Auntie?" He behaved just like an adult male on social occasions. Xiaoyu took to him right away.

Xiaoyu then said to Renyan, "Women in the alleyway are so fortunate, they use furniture passed down from their ancestors, their men are making good money and their children are healthy and sophisticated beyond words." Over the phone, she couldn't suppress her heartfelt envy.

"There are less fortunate ones and they have their share of difficulties. I would venture that Mother Zhang's days are rather difficult. Look how often she has to run up and down those set of stairs, she wouldn't let her eyes off even the bottle of soy sauce. Is it possible that she is guarding against you as well?" said Renyan as if he was deliberately pouring cold water on Xiaoyu.

"Don't you ever judge others with your distorted mind," Xiaoyu spoke coyly in a tone of a movie star. In front of Renyan, Xiaoyu was a proud person, but she would occasionally say or do something not exactly rational on purpose.

Downstairs, Huang Jiajia returned to the wing-room to talk to Jin Ming as soon as Tianye went to bed.

"Are you still watching sports?" She tried to grab the remote.

"The TV will be all yours 30 minutes from now, be a good friend, please." Jin Ming was trying to hold on to the remote.

"But I want to watch VCD now," said Huang Jiajia as she tried to switch the channel and have it her way.

"I beg you, will you please not block my view? Come, come over here, let me hold you in my arms." Jin Ming was doing his best to please Huang Jiajia.

"Are you trying to seduce me?" Huang Jiajia jokingly hit his stretched hand and laughed.

Tianye who supposedly fell asleep in the front living room opened his eyes the minute his mother left. After listening for movements in the neighboring room, he stole out of bed, lowered his body and tiptoed across the wing-room. As he was making his way, Tianye was hit by a coat Jin Ming had thrown that missed a small table as he took Huang Jiajia into his arms. He didn't even realize that the coat missed the table and hit Tianye instead. So, with the coat Tianye made his way upstairs surreptitiously.

Xiaoyu was on the phone with Renyan when she heard knocking at the door. Upon opening the door, she saw Tianye standing there. The little guy politely asked in a low voice, "Garret Auntie, can you spare ten minutes of your time to play with me?" A flattered Xiaoyu immediately forgot about Renyan and turned her attention to Tianye. Renyan hollered several times from the other end of the line, and finally hung up in frustration after getting no response.

"My Mom and Dad are doing what they do in adult movies. Look, just like this, they kept kissing each other. So I slipped out. You wouldn't sell me out to my Mom, would you?" Tianye was sitting on Xiaoyu's bed with a pillow pressed against his chest and demonstrating the scene to Xiaoyu. Surprised and amused by Tianye, Xiaoyu mussed her head and said, "Ok, I promise you I won't tell."

"Garret Auntie, are you married?"

"No."

"Neither am I. I don't want to get married. I would like to stay single. Singles tend to have white ticks."

"My goodness, ticks are dirty! Why do you like ticks?" Xiaoyu couldn't suppress her laugh.

"White ticks is a slang word for money. That is how kids in our school refer to money these days. Ours is an open society now. Dad says that in the future human beings can even be cloned, you don't need a mate to have a child, and no one will bother to get married anymore. Dad says that getting married is a fairly complicated thing. Auntie, I just want to clone a female Tianye, exactly the same as I am. What do you think of my idea?"

"Well, I don't know if a man can have an opposite sex clone. Maybe with future developments in science, your dreams may come true." Feeling that she was having a hard time catching up with him, Xiaoyu wondered what this kid would be like when grown up.

"What would my clone call me? Dad or Mom?" Tianye was apparently stumped.

"Well, let your clone call you 'Mom,' that could be fun," said Xiaoyu as she chuckled at her own suggestion.

"I would rather settle for Dad. It is too much trouble to be a woman. For a few days every month ..." Tianye started mimicking the voice in a TV ad for sanitary pads. Tickled and surprised, Xiaoyu said, "You are something, quite something." Then she started tickling him to stop him from continuing his mocking.

"Ten minutes is up. I need to go back to sleep. Auntie, am I a good man?" Tianye suddenly jumped down from her bed and wanted to go home, but not before throwing another interesting question at her.

"Oh yeah. You kept to your promised time and you are decisive so you're a good man." Xiaoyu nodded with a smile and helped Tianye put on Jin Ming's coat.

"I am going back to the kindergarten tomorrow. When I am back home next week, I will tell you about the extra-marital affair of my teacher." Tianye threw in another shocking cliffhanger at Xiaoyu as he was leaving.

Stunned, Xiaoyu wondered why a child growing up in an old-styled stone house seem like such a wild child.

Xiaoyu's classmate Little Monkey was the matchmaker who brought Xiaoyu and Renyan together. Her vivacious personality and her last name Hou (which is a homophone of *hou* for monkey), earned her the nickname back in her school days. After graduation, she worked as a marketing director at a real estate agency. She made more money than Xiaoyu, but she had a very busy schedule, sometimes flying into two or three different cities in one day. Little Monkey also studied German at a language institute at night. She said that Bonn was the German city she wanted to go the most, since it was Beethoven's hometown and a world famous college town known for its tranquility and grace.

Little Monkey came to visit Xiaoyu in an eye-catching Firebird sports car. She had the car parked right underneath Xiaoyu's window, hogging up most of the space of the narrow alleyway. Hearing Little Monkey's call, Xiaoyu poked her head out from the window and was shocked at seeing the car. She ran downstairs right away.

"Where did you get this expensive car? Did you steal it?"

Xiaoyu asked in a whisper.

"You should know me better than that. I would never get involved with stolen goods. I borrowed the car from a friend, just for fun. So, are you ready to join me for a spin on the highway?" Apparently not offended, Little Monkey was still all smiles after Xiaoyu's question.

"Why don't you come in to my garret apartment for a few minutes? I need to change my outfit anyway. Wait, you have to park your car first and remove the license plate," said Xiaoyu. She found a spot for the car at the turn of the alleyway and paid a neighborhood boy to keep an eye on the car at an agreed fee of ten yuan.

"Wow, look at the way you minded the details, you do act like you were my wife," commented Little Monkey with a laugh. Back in college, Xiaoyu and Little Monkey were inseparable. When you saw one of them, the other one was never that far away. Xiaoyu was also the one who made sure that they ate and were clothed properly according to season. Someone then jokingly started calling Xiaoyu Little Monkey's wife.

The first thing Little Monkey did was look around like a detective searching for clues. She then asked with a puzzled look, "How come I don't see a shaver or men's briefs?" Recovering from her initial surprise, Xiaoyu soon got the gist of Little Monkey's question. She howled and pressed Little Monkey to her bed, striking and denouncing Little Monkey with all of her might.

"So, Renyan doesn't live here? I thought your moving into the stone gate housing was an elopement for love." Little Monkey found her comment so hilarious that she pleaded to Xiaoyu for forgiveness.

"Where did you get that idea in your head? How come you just acted like my Mom? She came to inspect as well. My Dad chose not to join her inspection tour, as he believes in the adage of 'see no evil.' Don't you people know that I am a good girl?" Xiaoyu fell on the bed laughing, but on second thought, she grabbed Little Monkey again, refusing to let her off the hook that easily. After some more fighting, they both laid down on bed facing up and started chatting for quite some time.

During their college days, two experts from the Shanghai Women's League came to their department for a discussion on the concept of virginity. Both experts were old maids; they tried their best to paint themselves as kind and sympathetic souls. The female students who spoke up all claimed that out of self-regard and self-respect, they would not have pre-marital sex with their boyfriends. Male students, on the other hand, claimed that although they had nothing against non-virgins, they would prefer their girlfriends to be virgins nonetheless. They reluctantly attributed this to their "feelings," which seemed like a betrayal of the ambivalence of modern youths with progressive thinking. These young men were unwilling to relinquish the selfish nature of men from the past.

Sitting together, Xiaoyu and Little Monkey kept quiet at first. They knew many of the students very well who had spoken up, the girls and especially boys, and they weren't so innocent. They had sexual experiences before and some of them were currently sexually active. Xiaoyu and Little Monkey exchanged a look like they wanted to call them out, but Xiaoyu decided instead to shake up conversation.

"I don't think being virgin is that important. If sex is what the one I love wants and also what I truly want, I don't see the need to go against nature to deny oneself the pleasure of sex. Of course, we should respect ourselves and respect others. Once you are in love, you should ask yourself: What is more important, virginity or love? The fact is, even if you succeed in saving your virginity, you may not succeed in saving your love. Your feelings will be hurt and this is unavoidable."

While Xiaoyu delivered her thoughts, the two old maids from the Women's League stared at her hard. At that moment, she was still her old self, the one her classmates knew so well. Yet they now all looked at her with palpable surprise, even disapproval, as if she were someone who recently dropped from the sky. They believed that there were things you could say in private as you wish. Then there were times that you could even go further and be more presumptuous, but this was definitely not the occasion.

Then Little Monkey chimed in. "Imagine that you were walking in a scorching hot desert and you were very thirsty. Then you found water, but you tried to suppress your thirst for water. I think that would be a very cruel thing to do. It's the same thing with sex. For two people who love each other, only the perfect integration of their bodies and souls can make their hearts fly. To my understanding, this thirst for flight and beautiful integration is a fleeting moment. Once you miss it, you will miss it forever." At this point, both women felt an elation from their rebellious remarks. They had succeeded in upsetting a well-planned and sanctimonious discussion.

After the meeting, both Xiaoyu and Little Monkey received unsigned notes with the same message: Are you a virgin? I am extremely thirsty for your "water." They tore the notes to pieces in disgust.

"Xiaoyu, are you thinking of having a chastity memorial arch erected for you? Do you still remember the two cadres from the Women's League? Our so-called women's experts were spinsters. You are not thinking of following in their footsteps, are you?" Lying on the small bed in the tiny apartment, Little Monkey couldn't figure out what Xiaoyu meant by being a good girl.

"Nah, I just feel that I am not ready yet to do certain things with Renyan. I don't know why myself. I get aroused when I am with him, but it seems like there is still something standing between us. Could it be that we are not meant to be, at least not yet?" Staring at the ceiling, Xiaoyu posed the question to Little Monkey and herself.

"Not meant to be? If Renyan underwent a sex change operation, you two would practically be exactly the same. You are so right for each other, you share the same love in life, the same taste, what else do you want?" said Little Monkey emphatically.

"I don't understand it myself. Little Monkey, what about you and yours truly? Are you enjoying your relationship?" Xiaoyu changed the subject. Little Monkey had an invisible boyfriend whose identification was still shrouded in mystery. Xiaoyu only caught a glimpse of his back once. A man with broad shoulders and probably of a certain age. Xiaoyu gathered that he could be a married man.

Little Monkey didn't immediately respond to the question.

"Take my advice and stay away from middle-aged men. They will only confuse us and will never choose us." Xiaoyu stared at Little Monkey with a cryptic smile on her face.

"I am not interested in middle-aged men. The qualities they represent: civilization, maturity, selfishness, narrow-mindedness, cheapness, elegance … are no longer their true qualities." Little Monkey shook her head, and then added with a cryptic smile, "I know what you are thinking right now, but you actually know nothing. I will tell you all one day, but not now."

"It's alright. You and I, we are close, but I also have secrets from you. Now, all that is in the past. With life we need to take it one step at a time," said Xiaoyu. She sat up to look for some snacks.

"Wouldn't that be wonderful if you were a man? I would then marry you and enjoy preserved fruits every day. And all the stinky men would have to keep their distance," said Little Monkey as she unwrapped the preserved fruits handed to her by Xiaoyu.

"Are you a lesbian? My boss, a German lady is a lesbian. She flies to Hong Kong every weekend to be with her partner there. Maybe only women can best understand women. It is impossible to share certain thoughts with men. For instance, Renyan wants to make love to me, but I don't have the same urge, and yet I want very much to have him around. There is simply no way that I can tell him exactly what my feelings are," said Xiaoyu. She climbed back to her bed and felt somewhat depressed after confessing to Little Monkey. Little Monkey patted Xiaoyu's cheeks with sympathy.

"Listen carefully, Xiaoyu," said Little Monkey in a serious tone. "There is a very pretty and fashionable girl, a filing clerk at my workplace. I think she is trying to lure Renyan away from you. If you really want to be with Renyan you should let go of yourself a little."

"Well, there are handsome young men going after me too," Xiaoyu declared in defiance.

"Be sure you wouldn't end up on the losing side for being careless. Just remember this, Renyan is your best choice, once you let him go you will lose him forever," said Little Monkey. She paused and asked, "The handsome young man you mentioned, is he from the same stone gate house? Wow, you became the love interest of someone the minute you moved in, you are indeed a sex kitten!"

"Are you a nosy parker? Keep your voice down." Xiaoyu reminded Little Monkey, "This is no place for secrets. You opened your big mouth, and others will immediately believe that I am a loose woman. The first time Mother Zhang of the second floor got a glimpse of Renyan, she acted as if she wanted to pry everything out of him." Xiaoyu imitated Mother Zhang's reaction for Little Monkey.

"Damn it, how can you stay at a place that leaves no room for personal freedom? Move out of this lousy garret apartment right away! I'll find a nice apartment for you with a reasonable rent ..." Little Monkey laughed and fell on the bed again.

"No, I don't want it. I moved here simply because I fell in love with the atmosphere of alleyway housing. After all, I am still single, and this is only temporary housing, not a place for newlyweds." Xiaoyu's argument was not without merit.

"Everybody seems quirky nowadays. Take you as an example, a perfectly normal person all of a sudden deciding to move to the alleyway. Another classmate of mine gave up a nice job and started traveling without a penny to his name. His plan was to work and travel at the same time and to see the whole world. I have another friend who chose to be a housewife after getting her master's degree. Then she filled her time surfing the Internet, sending email, and making numerous friends on the web. She could hardly find time to cook. I am the only one who sticks to the old rules. I am making a lot of money and have no time to spend it. I also need to think of something different to enjoy myself," Little Monkey declared.

Xiaoyu didn't respond. Xiaoyu knew that Little Monkey was a hard worker and now a marketing director of the company. Although quite accomplished already, she would one day outperform many men and would never give up her career lightly.

Gradually, Xiaoyu came to know that people in the alleyway sometimes referred to the living room as dining room. Also, the couple's sitting room was simply referred to as a room, and generally off limits to others. And of course, these were the rules applied to households with larger than average spaces. For the majority of the households, rooms were multi-functional and there was no clear division of living room, bedroom and dining room. This was true to Xiaoyu's garret apartment, and the apartment of Mother Zhang as well. The old couple and their grandson Jilin all lived in one room in the front. Fortunately, Father Zhang didn't come home often.

The alleyway was at the height of its activities in the mornings and evenings. Most of the doors were kept open or ajar, and sounds traveled easily between apartments. Those who kept their doors tightly closed would automatically be regarded as weird. At the advice of Mother Zhang, Xiaoyu hung a half curtain at the entrance of her garret apartment. The curtain would not impede the airflow, but would somewhat block the view and extra efforts would be needed to have a good look of the outside or the inside. Xiaoyu would later learn that such a curtain was one of the features unique to the old-fashioned stone gate house.

One day, Xiaoyu got a glimpse of Jilin, the grandson of

Mother Zhang. Jilin was a twenty-year-old big boy. He happened to come up stairs when Xiaoyu was having a conversation with Mother Zhang. When he saw Mother Zhang he called out "Grandma." Mother Zhang asked if he ate breakfast, Jilin answered that he had it at the restaurant. Looking at Xiaoyu, he moved his lips, but nothing came out of him. As he was about to walk away, Mother Zhang stopped him, "Jilin, where are your manners? This is Sister Xiaoyu who just moved in, she is a translator at a foreign corporation, white-collared, and has a great future." Her dissatisfaction with Jilin was palpable from her voice and tone.

Feeling embarrassed, he nodded at Xiaoyu and bee lined towards the front apartment without uttering another word. Mother Zhang sighed and started talking about her family, "He is my grandson. No one knows what's going on in his young mind. I was the one who brought him up. His parents had been sent to work in the countryside in Jilin, a province in northeast China. After he was born, they thrust him under my care. A couple of years ago, they managed to move back to Shanghai, but they made no mention of having him back, and he doesn't want to reunite with them either."

At this juncture Jilin poked his head and called out for grandma. Judging from his voice, Jilin seemed to think that his grandma had been talking too much. Mother Zhang turned and told him to get some sleep, then chose to continue her conversation with Xiaoyu.

"Jilin attended the school of tourism the year before and is now tending bars as an intern at the Baihua Hotel. He has been working very hard, but has not yet received a formal offer from the hotel. I have 'taken care of' the family of the hotel manager. I only hope that the money was well spent and we won't end up empty-handed." Mother Zhang was apparently caten up by worry.

"It is indeed difficult to find a job nowadays. But Jilin is young and he seems smart as well, and bar tenders are very much sought after," said Xiaoyu, trying to put things in a positive light. She could sense that Jilin was not in a good mood. But Mother Zhang didn't seem to get her point.

"You don't know him, Jilin is too laid back. Like threading bean curd with a cotton yarn, it is impossible to lift it up. With all our efforts, he still can't take care of himself. I must have done something wrong to his family in my previous life. Since it was I who raised him all these years, he is not close to his parents or his sister. His mother is now working as the dishwasher at my son's restaurant. Life has been hard on her, too." As those words poured out of her mouth, Mother Zhang looked tired and weary. Xiaoyu nodded wistfully. Jilin again poked his head and called out for grandma. Mother Zhang shook her head and shut up.

Later when Jilin passed the garret apartment on his way out, he covered his face with a piece of folded newspaper and hurried downstairs. He didn't have the nerve to face Xiaoyu after his grandma's airing of the dirty laundry in public. At first, Xiaoyu found this rather amusing and laughed in the privacy of her apartment. Then she turned sober and fell silent. Jilin had made a very good and sympathetic impression on her.

Renyan called and asked how she doing. "Excellent," Xiaoyu responded. "I had a feeling like I live in a big family. There is also a lovely big boy. His parents moved to the countryside decades ago to work even though they were educated. He's very shy and sensitive, his name is Jilin."

Renyan cautioned her not to get involved in a triangular relationship. Xiaoyu dismissed the thought with a laugh, "I feel him the same way I feel about Tianye. To tell you the truth, he is not as mature as Tianye."

Renyan said, "You seem to have yourself well protected now. If you really want others to be your boyfriend, you need to get my permission." "It's a promise," said Xiaoyu.

It was two days later when Xiaoyu caught the sight of Jilin's mother. She was fetching water from the tap downstairs when she saw a sallow-looking middle-aged woman entering the building. When she first set her eyes on Xiaoyu, the woman seemed a little startled and then rushed upstairs without saying a word. As Xiaoyu got the water and took the electric kettle up, the sound of a woman crying could be heard from Mother Zhang's place.

"Everyday, the very sight of the dirty dishes piling sky high numbs me. Where do I start? I don't get any rest from morning till night. You see what it did to my two hands. They look absolutely terrible. And yet they still refuse to buy a dishwasher. Who would have thought that my own sister-in-law could be so heartless, more so than the capitalists before liberation? She snipes at me, too. I can't take it anymore," said Mother Zhang's sobbing daughter.

"Can't you just bite the bullet? Jobs are hard to come by nowadays. With so much unemployment, people would line up for jobs of washing dishes! As to the heartless woman, I will call your brother and have a talk with him." Mother Zhang's words were self-contradictory. She must be fuming as well.

"That's no use, don't you know what kind of person he is? He would jump up the second you poke him. With the pillow talk from that woman, he had lost his patience with me long time ago. He wouldn't listen to you. How is Jilin now? Being a hotel intern, is he receiving some kind of subsidy or compensation? You must keep an eye on him. There are too many drug users around, I am worried he might get involved with the wrong crowd. Ask him to turn in the money he makes," she said.

"How could I ask for the mere three or four hundred yuan he takes in? It isn't even enough to buy a pair of name-brand sneakers. You don't want to squeeze him into a corner, do you? If you are so worried, you can take him back. Just like a shoulder pole can in no way stand the weight of a bridge, I don't think I am in a position to assume all these responsibilities." Mother Zhang sounded somewhat offended.

"I know you would read too much into it, is this a taboo subject? Every member of this family is untouchable, except me. Everyone can ride roughshod over me!" The woman started crying again.

"Why, you idiot! Have I ever mistreated you? I have been the one who takes care of Jilin. Have you ever fed or clothed him? And I was the one who waited for him outside with a cold drink during the entrance exams. Come to think of it, why should I have bothered?" Mother Zhang was choked with tears.

"You asked for it. Why did you send me to Jilin Province in the first place? It was such a lousy bitter-cold place, where your ears or nose could fall off in deep freeze. I now have no place of my own and have to cramp into a tiny borrowed space worse than a pig's sty. I have no choice but to place my son here with you, we don't even have a refrigerator of our own, my situation is worse than everyone." Xiaoyu then heard the sound of the woman opening the refrigerator in disgust.

"You are the one who volunteered to go. Don't go around assigning blame. If there is anyone to blame, blame yourself." Mother Zhang sounded less confident now.

"I was only 15 at the time, what did I know? And why didn't you try to stop me?" The woman sounded very angry. Mother Zhang chose to keep her silence. All of a sudden, both women gave in to crying.

Xiaoyu's eyes teared up. She didn't want to listen in, but couldn't stop the conversation from wafting into her garret apartment. She thought of closing the door, but didn't want to appear impolite. How could you close the door the minute your neighbor has a visitor? She was a reluctant fly on the wall. She soon realized that the woman was the mother of Jilin. Xiaoyu had sympathy for the educated youth who went to the countryside decades ago, and yet she was ambivalent about her emotional outburst. She might be going through a difficult patch, but why having it out at her own mother?

Then again, isn't it true that you can get away with anything only with your mother?

Mother Zhang was an excellent cook. On the weekends, she

would be busy preparing meals in the shared kitchen while her man, who was referred to as Uncle Zhang by everyone, would sit by the back entrance of the alleyway and chat with neighbors at the top of his lungs. The voice would travel directly to the window of the garret apartment.

"Uncle Zhang, it's time for you to enjoy life. Why do you keep on working at your age?"

"Well, money can be spent on food and clothing. After all those years of work, my hands are still clean. There is no point of idling at home, and if a man is to spend all his time with the grandmas and moms of the alleyway, he will surely get sick."

"Why not keep company with Mother Zhang, you two could go out on a trip. You couldn't afford to be romantic while young, why not enjoy yourselves in old age?"

Mother Zhang responded from the kitchen, "Well, we are way beyond the age of being romantic. I am used to the life of doing household chores and cooking. As long as Mr. Zhang is in good health, enjoys eating and has no trouble sleeping, I'll be satisfied." She always referred to her husband as "Mr. Zhang" in front of others. From her tone, one could detect a deep sense of pride and the sentiment of the old Shanghai.

"Mother Zhang, Auntie Wang who lives in the back apartment of No. 27 is more open-minded than you are. She is now in a love triangle, several old men are fighting for her attention. A rich geezer even tried to seduce her by showing his passbook in US dollars, and to no avail. She is about the same age as you are, and enjoys her time in Suzhou or Hangzhou cities every now and then. And she couldn't be happier."

"Cows are fed on rice stalks, ducks on grain, we all go our separate ways. Having no husband, Auntie Wang in No. 27 can afford to be a free spirit. I can't. If I did let go of myself, I might have affairs. If I had affairs, Mr. Zhang would go crazy."

Xiaoyu liked how she insisted on calling him Mr. Zhang. It was a pleasure to hear an old lady referring to her husband that way. The audience was immediately transported to the alleyway days of the 1930s when all those who lived there were the middle-class, well-to-do families.

According to Mother Zhang, Uncle Zhang had been a bookkeeper in traditional Chinese robes before 1949. Now in his 70s, Uncle Zhang still worked at a township enterprise somewhere in Zhejiang Province and would come home to his wife on weekends. Uncle Zhang was a man of the older generation, who was served and cared for by his wife, seemingly the master of the household. But Xiaoyu felt that Mother Zhang was actually the one whom you have to reckon with.

Feeling bored one evening, Xiaoyu suddenly realized that all men in the building were not around. Uncle Zhang was working somewhere else; Jin Ming went to a bar that caters to football fans, where rumor has it that Xie Hui (a star football player) would show up from time to time; Tianye was "working" at his kindergarten; and as for Jilin, Mother Zhang suspected that he was in love since he acted lately as if he had lost his soul. A boy in love would surely not stay put at home. A thought crossed Xiaoyu's mind, maybe women were the real watchers of the old-fashioned stone house?

On Sunday, Renyan brought a computer over. Once the wires were hooked up, he started playing computer games right away. Xiaoyu began taking out cardboard boxes.

"You have turned my bedroom into a computer room, there is no atmosphere anymore." Xiaoyu was in the midst of tidying up the tangled wires.

"What atmosphere? You need to tone down the modern ambience. Look here, in a short while the man and the woman will take off all their clothes, just like in the British movie *The Full Monty*. Now, take a closer look. Do they look like someone we know?" said Renyan in a suggestive tone. While Renyan was busy punching away at the keyboard, the two people on the computer screen were strip dancing.

Xiaoyu turned to look at the computer screen, and was

immediately aback. The woman in the two-piece swimming suit looked exactly like Xiaoyu, and the muscular man, his small eyes opened wide, with nothing but a tiny brief on, looked exactly like Renyan at his most shameless. Renyan had apparently photoshopped their faces onto the disgusting dancers.

"Are you out of your mind? You dirty pervert!" Xiaoyu cried out in protest. She hit the delete key and unplugged the computer. Renyan slumped into his seat in frustration.

"The golden boy and the jade girl, Romeo and Juliet, the butterfly match of Liang Shanbo and Zhu Yingtai, they were all killed by you," recited Renyan in a loud voice with exaggerated grief.

"I could have killed you." Angrily, Xiaoyu picked up the computer and threw it outside. When she was about to show Renyan the exit, she turned and saw Mother Zhang come out of her apartment. She stopped at the door and stared at Xiaoyu.

"Miss, you just moved in, and you are about to move out now?" Mother Zhang seemed genuinely surprised to see the computer and the cardboard boxes scattered near the entrance of Xiaoyu's apartment.

"Oh, no, no, I was just cleaning up my room and I am done now." After making up an excuse on the spot, Xiaoyu was forced to take the computer and the boxes back in to cover up her lie. While Renyan jumped with glee inside the apartment, Xiaoyu was still miffed by what has just happened. Yet she had no choice, but to suppress her anger. All she could do was bare her teeth at Renyan.

Xiaoyu and Renyan soon made up. Renyan proposed to use the computer to watch a VCD, and Xiaoyu went downstairs to borrow one from Huang Jiajia. Huang Jiajia was not in, she was out with Tianye to celebrate his birthday at KFC. Jin Ming was home eating dinner alone and detained Xiaoyu for a while for some idle chat.

Jin Ming said that he overate last night while dining with his clients, so he chose to stay home. Besides, a live broadcast of the football match would be on in the afternoon. "Ever since crazy and overzealous fans stripped off my clothes simply because I was wearing a T-shirt with the opposing team's name on it, I dare not watch a game on site anymore," Jin Ming explained.

"That is so incredible, so incredible," Xiaoyu commented with a laugh as she looked through their VCD collection. Xiaoyu was deeply touched when she saw that Jin Ming was using a half piece of old paper to collect dinner scraps to keep the dining table clean.

She ended up settling on a movie since she thought Renyan might even like it. Still trying to make up for his behavior earlier, Renyan offered to leave his computer there just in case Xiaoyu wanted to watch more VCDs later.

Later when Xiaoyu relayed Jin Ming's particularly careful and considerate manners to her male colleagues, they were not as impressed. Recruited from other provinces, they were excellent workers at their respective positions, but a bunch of macho-like men who didn't care much about appearances. "What a sissy!" they sneered. From then on, the sight of her co-workers' messy desks always reminded Xiaoyu of Jin Ming's attention to detail. Then the embarrassing image of him being stripped of his clothes at the ballfield never failed to bring a smile to her face.

Upon learning that Xiaoyu had a computer, Tianye sneaked into Xiaoyu's garret apartment with a game and played his heart out. He was a computer whiz kid in spite of his tender age. He said that every Saturday, his Dad would accompany him to a computer class at a nearby school. Like many boys of his age group, they used class time to play computer games. They played MUD martial arts games and roamed to many different places. He claimed that he was considered an "evil player" on the network, and was looking for other great players for a match. With limited computer skills of their own, the teachers of this profit-minded school chose to admit defeat and gave these kids with "superior skills" a free rein in class.

"Your dad doesn't know about this?" Xiaoyu asked.

"Keep your voice down," Tianye reminded her. Xiaoyu stuck her tongue out in embarrassment. Tianye responded by mischievously sticking his neck out. "I have no idea where he goes when I am in class, he only shows up when my time is up. He bought my silence so I would never tell this to my Mom." Tianye raised his head and remarked proudly.

"You took a bribe at this young of an age? Oh, the time is up, you should go home now." With a smile, Xiaoyu urged him to leave. Tianye patted his own head, slid down the chair, and sneaked back.

"The fact that I took the bribe may not be strictly legal, but I didn't break the law either." With a wicked smile, the kid turned around and added.

At the back entrance of her building, Xiaoyu saw Auntie Wang who lived in No. 27, the one who was rumored to have many boyfriends. She was sitting in front of her apartment and perusing something with her reading glasses on. She had heard that Auntie Wang's husband disappeared not long after their marriage. She never remarried, had no children, and was leading a carefree life.

"Little Wang, are you reading something?" asked an old man half-heartedly while sauntered by. Then he stooped in a little to take some initiative. Auntie Wang responded vaguely, showing no interest in continuing the conversation. Xiaoyu laughed silently to herself when the old man then looked deflated and dragged his feet as he walked away from Auntie Wang. Love apparently makes no difference with age. When the old man finally left reluctantly, Xiaoyu approached the old lady and said hello out of curiosity.

Posing as an alleyway girl eager for a chat, Xiaoyu said, "Auntie Wang, are you reading a book?"

"Oh, it's you, younger sister. I was just browsing." Seeing that it was Xiaoyu, who asked the question, Auntie Wang broke into a polite smile. To Xiaoyu, Auntie Wang in her 60s still looked quite attractive: She kept her figure well, dressed appropriately, her skin tone was on the light side, and her eyes still sparkled. She always looked neat and tidy, as if she was dressed for an occasion every day.

What stood out in particular was her Chinese style tie-dyed jacket in blue, the color was pure and the workmanship impeccable. Xiaoyu felt that it would stand its ground even among the pieces in Esprit's window display. To her surprise, she also discovered that the reading material Auntie Wang was holding in her hands turned out to be a modern women's magazine *Models and Fashion*, and the article she was reading happened to be: *How to Keep Women Forever Young*. "No wonder so many old men were pursuing Auntie Wang," Xiaoyu mused.

"Auntie Wang, the jacket you are wearing is so exquisite. It's nice enough to be on the magazine cover. Where did you buy it?" said Xiaoyu in a sincere way.

"There is an old tailor nearby in the next alleyway, I have used him for several decades now. He was the one who provided me with the fabric. He used to make clothes for movie stars. I can introduce him to you if you wish." Auntie Wang sounded very enthusiastic.

Xiaoyu had no idea that you could still find tailors with such extraordinary skills in the small alleyways of Shanghai, she couldn't suppress her excitement and readily agreed to pay him a visit with Auntie Wang. Legend had it that there were also first-rate tailors hidden among the small streets of Italy. From time to time, international movie stars or socialites would come in, have their one-of-a-kind haute couture made there without fanfare, and would cause a splash in the fashion scene when they wore them out. With her own soon-to-be splash in mind, Xiaoyu shared her plethora of ideas with Auntie Wang and ended up lending the old lady her treasured fashion magazines.

Mother Zhang told Xiaoyu that Auntie Wang worked for a foreign bank when she was young, and her husband went to Taiwan soon after their marriage. She learned only a couple of years ago that her husband had died.

"But the news didn't strike Wang particularly hard at all. She said that her husband was no more than a stranger to her and didn't appear to be grief-stricken. In fact, there have always been men hovering around her," Mother Zhang mused, as if implying that Auntie Wang was a dissolute woman.

But Xiaoyu very much understood that feelings would inevitably fade with the passage of time. While in school, she resented the famous classic quote from the Song Dynasty (960 1279) poet Qin Guan, "If theirs is a love for life, not staying together night and day, they could still keep that love alive." She thought it was against human nature. But how could she explain it to Mother Zhang?

Mother Zhang also dropped a secret. She said that Auntie Wang actually had a thing for Uncle Zhang. She praised him as a real gentleman and liked to call him "Mr. Clinton" due to his resemblance to the president. Hearing the story, Xiaoyu laughed and thought that Mother Zhang had a big heart.

"Our Mr. Zhang had a wandering eye while young, but mended his ways as he aged. I am not jealous. In the past, Wang helped me handle my savings when she worked at a foreign bank. I had some money set aside when I was young, but it was gone within a few decades. In the years when Jilin's mother worked in the countryside in Jilin Province, I was so desperate that I almost sold my rosewood cupboard. It has now been passed on to my son. Well, as they say, you didn't come into this world with these goods, so you can't bring them with you when you go." Mother Zhang's resignation was tinged with bitterness.

"Mother Zhang, I don't think I ever met your son, right?" Xiaoyu asked.

"Oh, him, he only shows up once in a thousand years. And just like the Monkey King, he can never sit on his butt long, even when he visits." In one sentence Mother Zhang managed to include both the lyrics of a hit song and an allegorical pun from the classics. Xiaoyu couldn't help, but give a little giggle.

"You cared for your son a lot, didn't you?" Xiaoyu could tell what was going through Mother Zhang's mind and came out with the question in a playful manner. Mother Zhang nodded and smiled in frustration.

"Once the sons get married, they soon forget about their mothers. At first, Mr. Zhang thought he could help out with their books, but the daughter-in-law declined the offer. Mr. Zhang had no choice but to work in Zhejiang Province, a long way from home. Alas, nowadays things are turned upside down. A son could refuse to have his father work for him? What can you say?" Mother Zhang heaved a heavy sigh. Looking at Mother Zhang in sympathy, Xiaoyu tried to picture her in her youth. Since Father Zhang used to wear traditional Chinese robes, Mother Zhang must been at least a clean-looking handsome girl. Age works like a terrible corrosive agent. For decades it slowly sucked away the rich and warm life of this alleyway woman, until she became desiccated, exhausted, and numb.

At a small party given by Lenny, the German engineer who was also Xiaoyu's boss, at a German bar on Tongren Road, Xiaoyu, Renyan and Little Monkey all showed up, along with several German colleagues and other Chinese friends. It was an informal occasion, nobody gave any speeches, and no one was forced to mingle with others. Under a halo of light near the bar counter, the tall figure of Lenny could be seen chatting with a blonde. Others were scattered in small groups, drinking beer and talking about their trade. Renyan was new to this party format, he asked Xiaoyu in a whisper if it was necessary to exchange a few pleasantries with her German boss. Xiaoyu assured him that it wasn't necessary. "The best exchange of pleasantries is for you to have a good time," she said.

In a tie-dyed jacket made by the tailor of the alleyway, Xiaoyu looked especially beautiful and attractive. Little Monkey was overcome with envy, and tried several times to pry the source of the jacket from Xiaoyu. Her response was always a cryptic "no comment" and a smile. That had annoyed Little Monkey so much, she was ready to punch Xiaoyu for an answer.

As far as young girls are concerned, their sartorial secrets are even more important than their love secrets.

Xiaoyu walked away after making sure that the two friends she brought with her were well settled with other party goers.

"I thought it would be like in the movies where the host would stand at the entrance to greet his guests, it turned out that it was nothing like that at all. I now feel absolutely at home. Foreigners are so carefree, we Chinese are sticklers," Renyan said to Little Monkey. When beers were passed around, Renyan got one for her and one for himself.

"There is no need to look down on yourself. We have our own culture and tradition. When I am ready to throw a party someday, I will be sure to give a long boring speech. People will never forget it and will never come to another one of my parties again!" vowed Little Monkey while sipping her beer. She couldn't help, but laugh at her own silly idea out loud.

"If you have a party, I will never miss it as long as you serve food and drink. You may deliver your long-winded speech. I will hear it, but I won't listen." As he uttered those words, he saw Xiaoyu approach her German boss, and say something to her. The German woman smiled, waved her hand at them, and together with Xiaoyu, came their way.

"Renyan, here's an opportunity for the conversation you were hoping for," Little Monkey sighed.

"Hi, I am Lenny, how do you do?" With her lousy Shanghainese, Lenny greeted them enthusiastically, shook hands with them, and kissed their cheeks. When Renyan kissed the cheeks of Lenny, he glanced at Xiaoyu in triumph. Xiaoyu managed to suppress herself from laughing.

"My friend here will give a party tomorrow and she wishes to invite you as well." Renyan thrust Little Monkey in front of him. Little Monkey had no choice, but to nod with some embarrassment, while furtively giving Renyan a hard kick. Renyan uttered a yelp.

"Are you ok?" Lenny asked with puzzlement.

"I am ok. I just saw someone I knew." Renyan waved as if he was greeting someone over at the bar. The guy at the bar waved back good-naturedly, and let out a loud "Hi." Little Monkey couldn't hold back anymore and burst out laughing. Her face looked so pure and naive.

"Miss, the pleasure is all mine, I will certainly be there at your party, but where will it be held?" Lenny's eyes were fixed at the laughing Little Monkey while she eagerly asked the question politely.

"But ..." Little Monkey was at a loss of what to do.

"Lenny, we can go together tomorrow." Xiaoyu's timely intervention was addressed to both Lenny and Little Monkey.

"Ok!" Lenny raised her hand in a triumphant gesture, sat down, and joined in the casual talk.

Having studied German for some time, Little Monkey didn't find conversing with Lenny particularly challenging. There were plenty of German things to talk about, castles, church buildings, the River Rhine, as well as authors like Goethe, Marx and Freud. Lenny was also interested in Chinese culture, and to everyone's surprise, she lived in alleyway housing, a more upscale one, of course. She also liked to collect antiques of Shanghai. Xiaoyu knew well that it was the result of a Shanghai gentleman's influence. On the wall of her apartment, you would find a Beauty brand cigarette poster of the old Shanghai. She had traditional style furniture as well: a bed chest, brass bed, dressing table, and old piano. She even had knickknacks on the dressing table, including a bamboo weaved basket and copper candlestick holder. This was how Lenny immersed herself in the old Shanghai.

Xiaoyu told Little Monkey that Lenny's place was actually quite famous among foreign businessmen in Shanghai. Many of the newly arrived foreign housewives often sought to get the sense of Chinese culture at Lenny's before they decorated their own places.

"You are welcome to be my house guests," said Lenny. She

left her address to both Little Monkey and Renyan, but her intense gaze lingered long on the face of Little Monkey. Everyone suddenly realized that Lenny's invitation was meant for Little Monkey only.

Once Lenny walked away, the trio of good friends made a fist sign that they all understood and started gossiping. Somewhat embarrassed, Little Monkey questioned Renyan if it was true that men didn't find her attractive. Renyan immediately denied that it, "You are like the Oriental Pearl Tower that men usually find beyond reach."

Glancing at Lenny's address with puzzlement, Little Monkey all of a sudden let out a scream. Both Xiaoyu and Renyan were startled enough to stand up and in suppressed voices they asked, "What's the matter?"

"Party! Party! You were the one who told Lenny about the non-existent party, what do I do now? Where is the party?" Little Monkey stared at Xiaoyu and Renyan in extreme distress.

"No big deal, you are making so much money and claim to have problems spending it. We can easily find a small bar for a get-together. You will certainly find Lenny to be a worthy friend," said Xiaoyu. She seemed to take pleasure in Little Monkey's plight.

"She is a lesbian, I refuse to be friends with her. You take care of everything then. I wash my hands." Little Monkey sounded like her mind was made up.

"If Lenny made a pass at you, you could refuse, but you cannot show your detain. In fact, you have nothing to worry about. As far as I know, Lenny is a faithful kind of lover." Xiaoyu smiled and tried to put Little Monkey at ease. It was obvious that she had a lot of respect for her boss.

"Ok, let me take care of the party, and you pay the bill?" Renyan was shamelessly counting his fingers in front of Little Monkey. Since they worked in the same company, and knew each other so well, they interacted more like friends of the same sex.

"Why are you so snobbish? Here, this is my card, the

password is the same last 6 digits of the card number." Little Monkey threw a credit card at Renyan and pointed at the card numbers.

"Perfect!" Renyan proudly raised his glass in tribute to Little Monkey. The three of them then had a couple more drinks before heading out.

The next day, Renyan used Little Monkey's credit card and invited his whole gang to a teahouse on Hengshan Road. The scale of the party even surprised Xiaoyu who accompanied Lenny to the place. As he paid the bill with Little Monkey's credit card, he was almost taken to the police station by the teahouse security personnel. It turned out that there was just 30 yuan left on the card. In the end, it was the generous Lenny who signed and paid the bill. Suffice it to say, this was an episode that had a lot to do with what happened later.

Xiaoyu was roused from her sleep by a thundering noise before dawn.

"You little devil, where the hell have you been? Tell me, do you know what time it is now?!" It was the voice of Uncle Zhang. Xiaoyu figured that Uncle Zhang was hollering with some kind of disciplinary tool like a rod or a knife in hand.

"Four o'clock." It was Jilin's timid voice.

"Grandma and I were so worried that we didn't sleep at all. Are you trying to kill us? Did you get yourself in trouble? Nowadays criminals are mostly young, just tell me, did you rob or kill someone? Just tell me! I will accompany you surrendering to police." Uncle Zhang yelled, and it sounded like he was also grappling with Jilin. A loud bang shocked followed which shocked Xiaoyu. It sounded as if some furniture was thrown to the ground.

Downstairs, Huang Jiajia and Jin Ming were also roused from their sleep. They got up and put on some clothes. Jin Ming wanted to go up, but was stopped by Huang Jiajia.

Mother Zhang's chimed in with softer tone that was filled

with deep-seated worry and reproach. "Why don't you let the kid speak for himself, why get yourself so excited? Jilin, where did you hang out tonight? Staying up so late away from home, you really went too far this time. Grandpa meant well, it's for your own good."

"What kid? He is twenty now, you are the one who spoiled him. What would you say to his mother if he indeed had got himself in trouble? I want to speak to his mother, why did she leave such an impossible kid to our care?" Uncle Zhang was heaping all the blame on his wife.

Mother Zhang kept her quiet. Later, Uncle Zhang continued his pressure tactics and probably physical abuse as well. Jin Ming's several attempts to go upstairs and intervene were all stopped by Huang Jiajia.

"Even upright officials may not be spared of domestic problems. Why bother to get involved in troubles of others? This is none of your business," Huang Jiajia cautioned Jin Ming at a low voice.

"What if someone's life is at stake? I don't understand this old man. The kid has sustained his physical abuse for 20 years. Times are different now, does he still believe in 'spare the rod, spoil the child'?" Not knowing what to do, Jin Ming was pacing around in frustration.

"Jin Ming, his grandma is there, what do you have to worry about? The old man is not the one who calls the shots, the grandma, like the matriarch of the Jia family in *Dreams of the Red Chamber*, is the one in charge," said Huang Jiajia. She couldn't understand why Jin Ming was so agitated.

"Jiajia, how could you still keep your cool, I am so worried I can barely keep my cool." The couple was whispering to each other back and forth. Huang Jiajia then deliberately elbowed the lower part of Jin Ming's body. Jin Ming gave out a low moan and tip-toed towards the public toilet next to the shared kitchen.

"I beg of you, why are you so stubborn? Can't you honestly tell us where you went and what did you did? You may get lenient treatment that way." Mother Zhang sounded as if she was about to cry. Downstairs, Huang Jiajia almost laughed when she heard Mother Zhang refer to the national policy towards criminals.

"I ... I went to a disco place for Luo Zhongxu's all-night concert." After dragging his feet for so long Jilin finally gave in, probably in response to the repeated pleas made by Mother Zhang. When Xiaoyu heard his confession, she breathed a sigh of relief. She didn't know herself why she worried so much for Jilin.

"A ticket to the disco costs 80 yuan. Are you the rich son of a tofu store owner? I warn you, never again. From now on, you also have to pay for your meals here!" Uncle Zhang vengefully added. Jilin was silent.

The next morning, Xiaoyu called out to Jilin in a hushed voice as he passed through her apartment on his way down. Jilin nodded and slowed down. Xiaoyu followed him downstairs, while keeping the conversation going.

"Jilin, do you like pop concerts? I will give you tickets when I have good ones. Next week, a Japanese singer is coming to perform in Shanghai." Xiaoyu meant to comfort him a little.

"Gosh, do I dare right after what I have been through at the hands of that old man? Oh, how I hate him. Sister Xiaoyu, there is something you must keep it from my Grandma. I intend to rent a place of my own, just like you do. I'd rather starve myself in order to save enough for rent." Jilin was pouring his heart out to Xiaoyu. By that time, they had reached the stone gate housing's back entrance.

Xiaoyu and Jilin walked out of the alleyway together. Things looked a little disorderly in the morning. Near the entrance, the owner of a little dim sum stand from Anhui Province was busy making pancakes in a greasy chef's hat. A dirty looking three or four-year-old kid was hovering around, and you couldn't tell if the child was a boy or a girl. Across the alleyway, a laid-off woman ran a stand selling magazines and newspapers. She had shared with Xiaoyu her experiences of being a water bearer, a nursing assistant, and a cleaning lady after becoming unemployed. She had indeed come a long way to be a newsstand owner. Xiaoyu stopped to buy a morning paper. When she turned around, a Santana from the alleyway entrance suddenly came into view, a man immediately got in, and the car sped away.

Xiaoyu thought the man looked familiar and then remembered that he was the plant manager with a mouth sore. He once swore that he had no intention to stay on as the head of the money-losing plant, and claimed he had worn out his shoes searching for employment for those who were laid off. Now it seemed that none of that was true. Xiaoyu became upset. Jilin, the unemployed woman, the lying plant manager, the stand owner from Anhui, and his kid had all become indelible images in her mind's eye. On this gray morning, they refused to go away.

"Jilin, if you really want to move out, you need to consult your mother." Remembering what Jilin told her earlier, she advised him to act prudently.

"My mother is even worse than Grandma. She is always complaining and nagging. Every time she sees me, she asks if I am into drugs. She also asked me to hand in my subsidies. All she cares about is money, just like Grandpa. I am so fed up with her. I can't stand it anymore, sometimes I wish I were really into drugs." Jilin only harbored animosity towards his mother. Apparently, there was not much left with the mother-son relationship.

"But your Mom has her difficulties as well, after all she always has your interest in mind." Knowing the confusion of young adults at this difficult age, Xiaoyu cast a sympathetic eye on Jilin. The haggard looking mother of Jilin, the frustrated Uncle Zhang, and Mother Zhang who liked to beat about the bush—they all loved Jilin in their own fretful, truculent, and convoluted way. Had it ever occurred to them that this kind of love was the most unbearable?

"She wants me to stay with Grandma so that I will have a financial stake in Grandma's place, isn't it obvious? I only care for my grandma. What annoys me the most though is how she always publicly praises the other kids who have made it, implying that I am no good. This is more painful for me than physical abuse. I have a younger sister, a fat, ugly, greedy, lazy bone sister who is the apple of my father's eye. The three of them are cramped in small living quarters, seemingly very happy. Every time I go back home, I feel like an intruding stranger." From the way he talked about other family members, it seemed like he wasn't close to any one of them.

"Jilin, I will introduce some of my friends to you and we can go out together. What else do you like to do? Bowling, going to Karaoke bars, or killing time at coffee bars?" Xiaoyu asked Jilin at the bus station. When the bus came, they parted ways.

Not long afterwards, Xiaoyu and Jilin went to see the movie *The American President* in Movie Town. It was an unexpected story of true love between a man and a woman with a huge age and social status difference. On their way to the cinema, Jilin mentioned out of the blue, he once had the girlfriend who was a supermarket cashier. It turned out that Jilin had already tasted rejection.

"She was fat with bowed legs, not at all good-looking. The only thing she had going for her was the fact that her parents were also sent to work in the countryside after graduation. I thought that I would date a girl like this because she would stay faithful to me. Little did I expect that even she would look down on me and reject me. That came to me as a total surprise," Jilin remarked with palpable anger. He stretched out his finger to scratch the wall as they walked. Xiaoyu noticed that he had scraped his finger and blood was coming out. Is it possible that he had given into self-abuse? Xiaoyu wondered.

"You are too young. Two years from now when you are more mature with social and work experience, you will find the girl who loves you. And I will be proud of you then," said Xiaoyu, sounding like an older sister. This is why she was a smart girl. Before socializing with the opposite sex, she always made sure that they each knew where they stood, so that there would be no misunderstanding or hard feelings later.

When they later sat in the theater, Jilin reached out for her hand. Xiaoyu seemed to know that Jilin would do that, and she clutched his hand without any compunction. She didn't regard hand-holding as something unusual. She once even danced cheek-to-cheek with other boys at a classmate's birthday party. But on most occasions Xiaoyu was more reserved and dignified, of course.

Jilin clutched Xiaoyu's hand. Jilin was smart, he knew from the very beginning that Xiaoyu treated him as a child, and the comfort she offered now was as natural as she quietly called him out in front of her garret apartment. He felt he now had a shoulder to lean on and someone he could share his feelings with.

When the female lead in the movie got drunk in an act of self-destruction, Jilin quietly told Xiaoyu, "I also wanted to give up." Xiaoyu nodded and said, "I know you wouldn't, you have the courage to keep on trying, just like the unemployed lady at the alleyway entrance." Jilin continued, "The lady has more of an objective in life, her kids or her family, and I don't. I am afraid."

Xiaoyu didn't respond. She felt that Jilin was too childish and he seemed to have an overdependency on women. Xiaoyu was not ready to win over the trust of someone almost totally unrelated to her, a common trait among white-collar young females who tend to be self-centered and proud. Xiaoyu came to regret her silence later.

After the movie, Xiaoyu hardly saw Jilin at all. Mother Zhang often complained to Xiaoyu that Jilin was wilder now. He would stay out all night or sleep at home all day when his grandpa was away. He also twice took money from her drawer. Mother Zhang didn't dare to let her husband know the truth.

"It seems that his staying here is not a good idea. He is beyond my control and I cannot answer for his actions. Every time his mother visits, he chooses to stay away and avoid any face-to-face contact with her. Miss, can you talk to him when you have the opportunity? He seems to like you. Alas, just like the monks know nothing of Taoism, no one knows the trouble other families are going through."

Mother Zhang shared these thoughts with Xiaoyu when she knew that no neighbors were around. Xiaoyu understood that Mother Zhang cared about her image and her confession to Xiaoyu about Jilin obviously was made in desperation. But what could Xiaoyu do?

At the beginning of summer, the alleyway always smelled of dampness. An odor of warm moisture permeated the old structure, tinged with a toothpaste-like sweetness. Xiaoyu didn't feel like staying home and decided to go shopping with Huang Jiajia. Huang Jiajia worked as a bookkeeper in the labor department of a department store on Huaihai Road. By the time they passed the building, it was already evening and both felt sore and tired from too much walking. Xiaoyu proposed to rest a bit at Huang Jiajia's office. After a little hesitation, Huang Jiajia finally told Xiaoyu that she had already been laid off. Only one person in her office was asked to go, and everyone agreed to decide by drawing lots. She was the unlucky one who was asked to "go."

"Nobody in the alleyway knows that I've been let go. Xiaoyu, you are the only exception," Huang Jiajia said in embarrassment.

"Rest assured, I am not going to tell anyone. Let's find a coffee place then." Xiaoyu felt guilty that she was the one who forced Huang Jiajia's hand. They sat down at a teahouse opened by someone from Taiwan. Xiaoyu didn't order the bubble tea with dubious flavors, she asked for a cup of water.

"This is nothing important. I am taking insurance training courses now and am expecting to get the agent qualification paper soon. I will be making my rounds on the street like a salesman. But I am thin-skinned and there are newspaper reports exposing insurance frauds. Jin Ming doesn't mind me being unemployed and promises to take care of me, but I refused. I am worried that I will become a housewife if I stay home too long." Huang Jiajia sipped her bubble tea and mused rather sadly. She felt a pinch of regret the minute Xiaoyu ordered a cup of water, comparing her own taste with Xiaoyu's. Was her choice more in tune of that of an ordinary, bland housewife?

"I think insurance is an honest business, everyone should be allowed to make money. If you put your money in the bank, do you suppose that the bank will manage it for free? I promise you that I will be your first client." Xiaoyu was trying gently to put Huang Jiajia at ease. Of course, Xiaoyu was not emulating Lei Feng, the modern day Chinese Samaritan. She worked for a foreign enterprise and was given the freedom to buy her own medical insurance. She might as well do Huang Jiajia a favor.

"Nowadays only educated people like you can understand insurance. With your words of encouragement, I am determined to stay in the business. As a matter of fact, education is also a must for a good insurance agent. He or she needs to dress, talk and conduct himself or herself properly. After a few days of training I have learned a lot as well," said Huang Jiajia.

"When I was working at the firm on Huaihai Road, I spent all my days in office. I knew nothing of the outside world and mistook slavishly following fashion for good taste. But now I know that wearing no makeup or wearing it without people knowing that you did is the trend for white-collared females of today. Look, the long fingernails are now gone." With wistful resignation, Huang Jiajia stretched out her hands for Xiaoyu to see. Indeed, the dream-like purple nail polish was no more, now her nails were cut short and in natural color, as if she was ready to turn a new leaf in life.

Xiaoyu also showed Huang Jiajia her own hands, Her fingernails were neatly trimmed, and they showed a natural youthful sparkle without the help of artificial embellishments. The two of them joyously clapped their hands and had become the best of friends who had no secrets from each other.

From Jin Ming, Xiaoyu learned that football was the one game men find the hardest to give up. On a Saturday afternoon, she was sitting on a stool chatting with Auntie Wang when she heard fighting at Huang Jiajia's place. It turned out that Tianye had a computer class at a school nearby and Jin Ming didn't want to go with him because of the live broadcast of a football match. Wearing light makeup and in a rather elegant suit, Huang Jiajia was in a hurry to go out, too. She wanted to meet with a client who was ready to buy health insurance. To the neighbors, her explanation for a change of profession from an office worker to an insurance agent was that she decided to "jump ship," a face-saving way of covering up the truth.

"I will pay you the insurance commission from this deal," said Jin Ming, who wanted her to accompany Tianye.

"I've talked to this person ten times and I've finally coaxed him into buying. I have to keep my part of the bargain." Huang Jiajia was in a rather good mood.

"Why did you use the word 'coax'? You are apparently not a qualified salesman." Jin Ming jabbed at her on purpose.

"I slipped, I didn't mean it really. Don't you dare use my words against me. Go, go, and be on your way. Tianye, keep an eye on your father, don't let him out of your sight." Huang Jiajia was advising Tianye instead of Jin Ming.

"My, my, who is the father here? Am I not allowed my personal freedom?" Jin Ming retorted with a wry smile.

"You lack self-awareness. As a kid, Tianye is aware enough to take computer lessons. What about you?" Huang Jiajia pointed at her rambunctious son who was eager to be on his way.

"Dad ..." Tianye winked at his Dad. When Jin Ming finally got it, he took Tianye's hand and they left together. Huang Jiajia smiled in satisfaction.

"Men are like that, they never grow up," said Huang Jiajia, standing at the back entrance to see Tianye and Jin Ming off the alleyway. Holding her head high like a professional, Huang Jiajia was ready to leave with her big attaché case. But her pager started beeping when she was only steps away from home. She hurriedly turned around and called the number back from her living room. A while later, Huang Jiajia in pajamas appeared and took Xiaoyu by surprise.

"This annoying client promised me that he would buy the insurance today, and now he says that he'll be out of town on business. I have been taken for a ride so many times by him. He must have a screw loose. It's been one month into the business, and I haven't even managed to complete one transaction. I am so desperate, sometimes I really wanted to give up and resign myself to be a housewife!" As she came to the water basin to wash the light makeup that she had so carefully put on, Huang Jiajia also vented about her frustrations with other clients. Jin Ming appeared at the back entrance. He didn't expect Huang Jiajia to be home, especially in pajamas. He thought she had no intention of going out, and appeared disappointed.

When Xiaoyu saw Jin Ming, he frantically signaled at her and Auntie Wang not to say anything. Then he stooped low and quickly slipped back in their apartment behind Huang Jiajia's back and never showed his face again. Xiaoyu learned later on that Jin Ming was hiding in their bedroom watching the football match with earphones. Luckily for him, Huang Jiajia kept busy between the kitchen and the living room and never even set foot in the bedroom after washing out her makeup.

For a change of pace, she later sat down with Xiaoyu and Auntie Wang to chat about tall stories surrounding insurance agents. One story went like this: An American agent depressed by his love life was about to jump off the Golden Gate Bridge, but the police came in time and stopped him. As he was describing his sad story to the police, his emotional state depressed the police so much that he and the policeman later jumped to their deaths together.

"A good insurance agent has to be a sweet talker. Whatever comes out between his upper and lower lips is always logical and reasonable. He can even talk the dead back to life. And yet, I am not like that at all," Huang Jiajia sighed.

"One day, when you acquire that eloquence, be sure not to commit suicide, or those who try to dissuade you will be in big trouble." Auntie Wang exhibited her sense of humor. Both Xiaoyu and Huang Jiajia roared out in laughter.

"No, I won't kill myself. I will go to the Yangpu Bridge looking for those who wish to commit suicide and ask them to pay me a lot of money for what I have to say. I will tell them that with a peaceful mind it's never too late to start a new life, and they will find even eating preserved vegetables an enjoyment."

"By your logic, I am ready to live to one hundred and fifty years old. Oh, Clinton is here." Seeing Uncle Zhang was walking towards them from afar, Auntie Wang cried out for him. Hearing her call right next to her, Xiaoyu could indeed sense her feelings for Uncle Zhang.

"Why sitting in rows, are you having a meeting?" Uncle Zhang politely nodded towards them, while keeping his distance. That immediately changed Auntie Wang's mood. Sizing up Uncle Zhang closely, his tall stature, full head of white hair and a decent bearing, Xiaoyu could see his resemblance to Clinton. He went inside after saying hello. Auntie Wang went silent for a while. Huang Jiajia winked a few times at Xiaoyu. Many knew of Auntie Wang's secret feelings for Uncle Zhang.

Auntie Wang stood up nonchalantly and returned home. As she walked away, Huang Jiajia muttered: "Unrequited love." Xiaoyu smiled and didn't say anything in response. In her heart, she had sympathy for Auntie Wang. It was at this juncture that Huang Jiajia said unexpectedly that she would like to go back home to watch *Titanic* on VCD, her most recent buy.

"You want to watch it with me?" Huang Jiajia extended her an invitation. Xiaoyu vigorously waved her hands in refusal, fearing what would happen if Huang Jiajia walked into the room and found Jin Ming there.

"*Titanic*'s director James Cameron once said that the small screen can in no way match the effect of the big screen. Why waste your time?" Xiaoyu anxiously tried to dissuade Huang Jiajia.

"I have nothing to do anyway, it's just a way to kill time until they come back." Huang Jiajia didn't know what was really on Xiaoyu's mind and went back to her bedroom anyway. Xiaoyu watched her every move carefully, wondering if she would be scared out of her wits once she found a man in her room. It was at that moment she heard a piercing scream of sheer terror from Huang Jiajia.

Xiaoyu immediately covered her ears.

Later, Huang Jiajia walked to the nearby school in dejection. Taking Jin Ming's place as the escort for Tianye, she soon found out the secret of Tianye. He was playing the role of the devil in the midst of a fierce fight with the martial arts masters from the schools of Shaolin and Wudang. It was too late by the time he turned his head and saw his mother.

"The two men I love the most in life betrayed me. I don't understand why they did that." A broken-hearted Huang Jiajia confessed to Xiaoyu. Looking sympathetic, Xiaoyu was also at a loss, why men would lie to their wives and mothers? In her train of thought, she was treating Tianye as a grown man, despite the fact that he was still at the tender age of six. Then again, Xiaoyu knew that a boy growing up in the alleyway was no ordinary boy.

As Huang Jiajia went to the living room to answer a phone call, Tianye told Xiaoyu in a pouty voice that he could no longer go to the computer class. "My mom formally withdrew me from the class right there." Needless to say, Tianye's teacher was left nonplussed and embarrassed.

"I will see you tonight. I will make sure my mom doesn't find out." After whispering these words to Xiaoyu's ear, Tianye swiftly darted into the alleyway for more horseplay. By the time Huang Jiajia came out, he was nowhere to be found.

Xiaoyu had been debating if she should spend the night at her mom's now since she had decided that she would leave Tianye disappointed.

"Jin Ming is still watching the football game, right now he doesn't know who I am anymore." Huang Jiajia was still fuming.

Xiaoyu didn't quite know what she meant.

"Come and take a look and you'll understand," said Huang Jiajia, dragging Xiaoyu to their bedroom. She saw Jin Ming sitting in front of the TV, earphones on his head, eyes glued to the screen without blinking, and not paying the slightest attention to Huang Jiajia or Xiaoyu. At that moment, he looked exactly like Tianye when playing computer games.

"Sir, I am an insurance agent, you seem to be a well-educated man, you must have bought insurance before, have you?" Before Huang Jiajia even finished her sentence at the bedroom door, Jin Ming came over and pushed her away. "Go, go, insurance is a fraud, I am unemployed, I have no money to buy insurance," Jin Ming said this without his eyes ever leaving the TV screen.

"I am not here as a salesman. I am here to raise your awareness. Listen, our society today is every man for himself. Everyone needs security, if not for yourself, you need to think for your wife, your son. Once you have the insurance, should something happen to you, your love can still be felt …" Huang Jiajia poured out her forceful and eloquent shoptalk, in an attempt to provoke Jin Ming.

Extremely annoyed by the distraction, he removed his headphones, ran into the kitchen, and threatened Huang Jiajia with a knife. "Are you leaving or not? If not, you will live to regret it," he said. Huang Jiajia said to him, "Look at me again, who am I?" Jin Ming stared at her and said, "The hell if I care who you are!"

At this juncture, the TV gave out a thundering roar, Jin Ming immediately returned to his TV seat and didn't let up with his wife. "You should buy yourself insurance, I might break your leg one day!" Huang Jiajia got so angry, she kept pounding on Jin Ming's shoulder, while screaming, "I am Jiajia, I am Jiajia!" Soon her screaming turned to sobbing.

Xiaoyu was dumbfounded by what she saw. She walked away not knowing what to say or do. While climbing the stairs, she could hear her every step on the creaky wooden staircase.

Thump, thump, thump with a squeak here and there. A sense of sadness overtook her.

Renyan would come to visit Xiaoyu every now and then. Late one night on his way out, Renyan unabashedly said to her while passing the shared kitchen, "I am not leaving, let me stay here overnight." Xiaoyu, refused, saying, "No marriage, no way." Renyan all of a sudden held her close and kissed her, even groping her breast. The building was so quiet. Xiaoyu, worried about the neighbors, would dare not to speak up, and let Renyan take advantage of her. Seizing the opportunity, Renyan tried to go even further, but Xiaoyu fought him off.

"Let's get married, we can go to the Bureau of Civil Affairs and line up for a marriage registration tomorrow before day break," Renyan murmured, anxious and impatient.

"I am not ready yet. Tianye said marriage is something very complicated. I'd have to agree with the kid," Xiaoyu murmured. Renyan's caressing had softened her original resistance and she became tender.

"What should we do then? Are you saying that we should register with Tianye? And Tianye might ask, what do you want, a male clone or a female clone?" Renyan found this at once preposterous and frustrating.

"You are getting warmer." Xiaoyu then covered her mouth and snickered. She moved to kiss Renyan, but by then he had lost his interest. He left in disappointment after making some perfunctory moves.

As expected, someone was listening on the other side of the wall. Huang Jiajia who lived downstairs was the first one to hear Xiaoyu uttering the words "no marriage, no way." She then said to Jin Ming, "I had no idea that she was a virtuous woman." Jin Ming said, "If Renyan tried to force himself on her, I would go punch him the minute Xiaoyu cried for help." Huang Jiajia retorted, "You just like to butt in on someone else's business. What about taking care of the wife of yours for a change?"

Jin Ming asked, "Are you asking for trouble? Don't you think that I take care of a lot of things around here already?" Huang Jiajia responded, "Oh yeah? Do you know my measurements, or the color of my panties?" Jin Ming shook his head in resignation, "You women are such nags."

Their mood darkened as they talked and argued, and then they heard the claque of the back door when Renyan left. In the dark, Huang Jiajia and Jin Ming exchanged a look. They regretted missing what went on between Xiaoyu and Renyan while they fought. They both inexplicably sighed and went back to sleep without another word.

Auntie Wang died peacefully. It turned out that Xiaoyu was the first one who made the discovery. Xiaoyu and Auntie Wang had agreed to pay a visit to the old tailor in the alleyway together. She first knocked on Auntie Wang's back door. Hearing no response and seeing that the door was not closed completely, she pushed her way as usual. She found Auntie Wang dozing on the square table with her face down. She gave her a little push. It was then that she realized that Auntie Wang was already dead.

Xiaoyu screamed and ran out, as she didn't know whom to ask for help. She ran to the back entrance of Building 12, her own building and called out for Jin Ming and Huang Jiajia. Little did she expect that they would panic more than Xiaoyu at the news and wouldn't even dare to enter Auntie Wang's apartment. One tried to poke from outside and the other disappeared on the excuse of phoning the police. At this moment, Xiaoyu finally calmed down, she walked around the body a few times and made an unexpected discovery. Auntie Wang actually had a picture in front of her, a picture of her and a man. It was apparently taken some time ago, but Xiaoyu could still tell that the man in the picture was no other than Uncle Zhang. So it was true that Auntie Wang and Uncle Zhang had a fling once. Xiaoyu hesitated a little before taking the picture to hide it.

The doctor concluded that she died of natural causes.

The unexpected death of Auntie Wang was the talk of the alleyway for quite some time. Some blamed it on the tortured TV soap operas. Some claimed that she had been waiting for a secretive boyfriend, fell in sleep while waiting, and then sunk into eternal sleep. Some old neighbors of a certain age wiped away tears when they heard the news, but the strange thing was that the old men who used to hover around Auntie Wang didn't seem to take the news especially hard. Whereas the old women seemed heartbroken by the loss, the one who shed the most tears was Mother Zhang.

"Wang always called Mr. Zhang Clinton. It was such a pity that she died alone and by herself," said Mother Zhang repeatedly to many neighbors. This was Mother Zhang's professed emotional state, and Xiaoyu's emotional state was in reaction to that of Mother Zhang. She wondered if Mother Zhang would still cry her heart out if she knew of the affair between Uncle Zhang and Auntie Wang. Xiaoyu also felt some unexplained resentment towards Uncle Zhang. He must have enjoyed being loved by two women at the same time. She had the urge of exposing him somehow.

Xiaoyu chose a time when no one was around to return Auntie Wang's picture to Uncle Zhang. She carefully observed the old man's every reaction. At first, Uncle Zhang was taken aback before politely offering Xiaoyu a beverage. She noticed his hand was slightly shaking when he opened the refrigerator door. Xiaoyu wondered then if her violation of his privacy was a bit cruel for an old man in his seventies.

"Maybe it was my fault. I just couldn't forget her, we became close friends in spite of our age difference," Xiaoyu explained how she got hold of the picture. Instead of referring Auntie Wang by name, she only used the pronoun, as they both knew who "she" was.

What happened afterwards took her by surprise. Uncle Zhang took out a cigarette lighter and set the picture on fire.

It burned slowly in the ashtray, the flames lit up Auntie Wang's beautiful face.

"You, why?" Xiaoyu looked at him, puzzled.

"She is gone. What's the use of it? Why couldn't she just let go? I don't get it." He stared at the flames, and the woman and the man in the flames, with resignation and with seemingly no emotion.

"You are right. For Auntie Wang, it was a waste of feelings, because there are things that do not deserve to be remembered," Xiaoyu said tongue in cheek, while coldly watching Uncle Zhang. He naturally understood what she was trying to say.

"Don't blame me. You are too young to understand. This is a secret between her and me, and my wife, the three of us. It happened long ago. You know that she was ... quite attractive. My wife found out after we were together a few times. She's a good wife and a classy lady and didn't raise hell or give me a hard time. She just wanted me to promise that it wouldn't happen again. We have kids, what else could I have done?" Uncle Zhang talked about the past without emotion, as if he was relating a story about another time, another person.

It was Auntie Wang who found it hard to let go, not while she was alive, nor while she was dying. And the one who ruled the fate for the three of them was Mother Zhang.

Xiaoyu remembered Mother Zhang once said that her Mr. Zhang had a wandering eye while young. Could it be that he had other affairs besides the one with Auntie Wang? Xiaoyu also remembered that Mother Zhang cried her eyes out at the news of Auntie Wang's death, saying that it was such a pity that she died alone. Xiaoyu figured that Uncle Zhang was at most an ordinary unfaithful man, but Mother Zhang was much more complicated. After this, she had an odd feeling every time she saw Mother Zhang's smile. She wondered how many stories of this alleyway were hidden behind that cryptic smile.

Jilin's drug addiction was found out by accident. It happened very late one night when Jilin was found having a seizure. Mother Zhang was so worried that she knocked on Xiaoyu's door. As Jilin struggled downstairs with their help, Jin Ming and his wife were awoken by the cluttering footsteps. Jin Ming came out and asked if they needed help. Jilin with difficulty burst out a loud "No!" Jin Ming and his wife looked at each other in surprise. Even Xiaoyu couldn't understand why the gentle Jilin would become so impatient and furious.

"He must have been tormented by his condition," she reasoned.

When Xiaoyu and Mother Zhang helped Jilin to the street to hail for a taxi, Jilin said, "I am not ill." Jilin fainted after a cry for his mother. At the hospital, they discovered his drug addiction. The hospital transferred him to a forced drug rehabilitation center. Jilin never protested.

On their way back from the rehabilitation center, Mother Zhang begged Xiaoyu in tears, "Please keep the matter to yourself. I have lived in the alleyway for decades. In my seventies, I don't want to be the talked about behind my back. I cannot live with the shame."

Moved by her tears, Xiaoyu agreed not to tell anyone. She knew that rips and tears were underneath Mother Zhang's superficial calm life.

"But Jin Ming and his wife are concerned about Jilin, they might even go to the hospital for a visit." Xiaoyu shared her worry with Mother Zhang. "Jilin would be gone for a whole month, and how could his long absence be covered up at this stone gate building."

"I will tell Jin Ming and his wife that Jilin had returned to live with his mother." Mother Zhang wiped away her tears and confidently assured Xiaoyu, who nodded with understanding. After returning to her garret apartment, she heard the heavy steps of Mother Zhang walking into the front part of the building. Xiaoyu realized that at this old stone gate building, this inconspicuous small old lady was actually a pivotal figure.

She decided not to go back to sleep after coming back to the first speck of breaking daylight. Leaning against the bed board, she felt a deep sense of guilt for what happened to Jilin.

"My Mom always worried that I would turn into a drug addict. I am so fed up with her, I can't stand it anymore. Sometimes I wish I were really into drugs. I only care for my grandma." Jilin had said as much. But no one actually thought he would embark down a road to drug dependency. Tears welled up in Xiaoyu's eye thinking about the pitiful look on Jilin's face when he uttered those words.

She also remembered the first time she set eyes on him. Out of shyness, he used a newspaper to cover his face. He once was so pure and naive. In fact, there were signs of his later drug use, such as staying at the disco deep into the night, disappointment with his surroundings, being rejected by his girlfriend, his shattered self-respect. He almost had no friends. She then realized that he had been trying to avoid her by quickening his steps when he went past her apartment. Jilin once regarded her as someone he could confide in, but Xiaoyu chose not to respond for whatever reason. If she had been more open and helpful at the time, maybe Jilin would not have gone this far?

Mother Zhang was knocking at the door while Xiaoyu was still deep in her thoughts.

"Miss, I am sorry. Would you come and sit in my front apartment for a while?" said Mother Zhang, her voice overwhelmed by worry. Xiaoyu immediately followed the elderly woman to the front apartment without saying a word. Upon entering the room, she saw that the mother of Jilin was already there. Her eyes were red, apparently from crying.

"I see no hope in life. Once Jilin is out, I will end our lives together with gas." She was absolutely hysterical. While sobbing, she complained about how hard she had to work at the restaurant run by her brother and sister-in-law, she didn't eat or sleep well, and she cried every day. In a short span of two years, worry had turned her hair white. She did all of this for Jilin, and now it was like drawing water with a sieve, it all came to nothing.

"You have to keep things in perspective. With no exception, life is like a rag, it has to be ready to absorb all tastes that fate delivers to it, be it sour, sweet, bitter or hot. The doctor said Jilin's case is not serious, and he could be rehabilitated. He is young and in good health, he should be able to pull through. Xiaoyu can confirm this, if you don't believe me. I am still looking forward to the day when I can enjoy being taken care of by Jilin." Mother Zhang angrily chided her daughter, her every word carried the weight of the old mother's feelings and concerns.

By now, Xiaoyu finally understood why Mother Zhang wanted her there. She was to talk some sense into Jilin's mother. Even without Jilin, his presence could still be felt everywhere in the room: tapes, CDs, Walkman, the magazine *Football World*, and the Japanese cartoon *Slam Dunk* ... everything that a healthy boy would love. Xiaoyu found it hard to believe that Jilin really went to the rehabilitation center.

"Auntie, this is the time that Jilin needs you the most. He even cried out for you on his way to the hospital." Xiaoyu started out with something general. She had never comforted others before. In the eyes of her generation, pain is considered the most private, hence inconsolable. But the minute she opened up, tears rolled down her cheeks. She couldn't tell if they were for Jilin or the woman who went to the countryside in her youth, or for Mother Zhang, the old woman who spent all her life in the alleyway.

"I worried that Jilin would reject me. He had avoided me, believing that I didn't care for him. In fact, it would've been difficult to have him live with us, my mom knows. I am renting a tiny mezzanine place where the owner moved out and is waiting for demolition compensation. How could I ask Jilin to move in with us? I didn't want to shortchange him ..." Her tears cascaded down.

"Alas, I didn't have my life properly handled. Not only has this affected the second generation, but the third generation. I must have done something wrong in my previous life since each generation is doing worse than the last ..." Mother Zhang broke down suddenly. Jilin's mother had been busy in wiping her own tears, she apparently didn't hear what her mother just said. But Xiaoyu understood the painful moments Mother Zhang went through.

"Auntie, may I suggest that you let Jilin stay with you after he comes out of the rehab and let his sister stay here with Grandma? He might get better under your care. Oh, it's about time for breakfast. May I go out and fetch some for you?" Xiaoyu found facing two women in tears was too much to bear.

Mother Zhang vigorously declined. Xiaoyu then fled the scene on the excuse that she needed to go to work. What she lacked in coping with the two sobbing women was not sympathy, but courage. Walking in the alleyway dappled with sunshine, Xiaoyu had lost her initial sense of freshness. She now felt that the alleyway had witnessed too many lives and too many misfortunes.

Jilin indeed returned to live with his mom. But the strange thing was that his sister didn't trade places with him at Mother Zhang's. Maybe their mother no longer trusted her parents, and was afraid the daughter would repeat the same mistake there. On the other hand, maybe these two elderly people dared not to take in the granddaughter. They didn't want to risk being blamed again should something happen to her, too.

Xiaoyu noticed that Mother Zhang was not as strong as before. One day, Mother Zhang told Xiaoyu that she had participated in a laughter club organized by the neighborhood for older people. Out of curiosity, Xiaoyu went with her to take a look. She saw a whole room of older women laughing for no good reason. Mother Zhang said that laughter could reduce your age by ten years. Looking at these old people who laughed for the sake of laughing, Xiaoyu wondered what the world had come to.

Little Monkey was going to Germany, and it was Xiaoyu's boss

Lenny who was paying her way. Lenny had come to the rescue the other night when Little Monkey played a joke on Renyan by giving him a bankcard that had almost no money in. The move almost had him landed in jail for committing fraud. When Little Monkey insisted on paying her back, the two women became fast friends. In Lenny's living room tastefully decorated with oriental art, they discussed Chinese culture and listened to German music.

As a precaution, Little Monkey's every visit to Lenny was accompanied by her boyfriend. She knew that this was not fair to Lenny, but she couldn't go against the custom. Fortunately, Lenny didn't seem to think that it was a precautionary measure by Little Monkey. She always received Little Monkey and her boyfriend with enthusiasm and without question. Aside from informal discussions and music, Lenny would often treat them with Western desserts served in an exquisitely made red lacquered antique basket. They had heard that Lenny would only use her beloved red lacquered basket for her closest friends.

When Lenny learned that Little Monkey was looking for an opportunity to study abroad. She quietly offered financial support. Little Monkey was touched by the gesture, but was not in a position to return the favor.

Before leaving, Little Monkey came to seriously bid farewell to Xiaoyu. Little Monkey suspected Xiaoyu had suspicions about her relationship with Lenny.

"Rest assured, nothing is going on between me and Lenny. I am not a lesbian. But Lenny is a true friend and an outstanding woman. I regret not being able to love her," said Little Monkey sincerely. The only unusual thing one could detect was a sense of sorrow in her eyes when she said that to Xiaoyu.

"Little Monkey, I would still be your best friend even if you were a lesbian. I will miss you." They gave each other an emotional hug. Xiaoyu didn't tell Little Monkey that Lenny had broken up with her lover in Hong Kong because of her. She knew that Little Monkey was not responsible for what happened, but she couldn't help but feel somewhat sorry for the kind-hearted Lenny. Maybe Little Monkey's departure would dampen Lenny's enthusiasm.

"My boyfriend said that, physically or psychologically, Lenny is more normal than any other woman." Little Monkey mentioned her boyfriend by accident.

"Exactly who is your boyfriend, whom I have never sets eyes on? I sometimes wonder if he exists at all." To satisfy her curiosity, Xiaoyu finally asked the question. She never asked it before because Little Monkey had been deliberately coy about it and she didn't want to impose. And on the eve of her going to a place far away, she couldn't resist the temptation anymore.

Little Monkey burst out laughing.

"Xiaoyu, you just nailed it. I actually don't have a boyfriend in that sense. I haven't found the right man yet and I don't want to settle just to be with someone. When the occasion called for it, I would just borrow someone. I borrowed my father when I went to go see Lenny. As far as Lenny is concerned, I owe her an apology." As the biggest secret of Little Monkey came out in the open, Xiaoyu found it both funny and sad.

Little Monkey became quiet after her roars of laughter. Indeed, how could you be in a good mood after you had lied to a dear friend who cared about you?

The lukewarm relationship between Xiaoyu and Renyan remained unchanged. His visits were now few and far in between. When Renyan did come by, he would spend his whole time playing computer games or talking with total strangers on the Internet about architectural style and design. Xiaoyu always got bored when Renyan discussed axis lines and golden sections on the Internet. She still missed him when he stayed away, and would invite him over. Renyan would always respond to her beckon call, Xiaoyu was sure about it. She didn't know that she would lose her hold on him one day.

Xiaoyu said, "This is not a game room, can't you do

something else with it?" Later, Xiaoyu decided to let him be the observer while she got online herself. At first, she meant it as retaliation to Renyan, but before she knew it, she found herself trapped and couldn't get away. One day in a chat room, she met a man named Hart, an American who claimed he was brought up on a Montana farm and owned a beautiful horse. Xiaoyu asked him if he had seen the movie *The Horse Whisperer* since the story took place in Montana. Hart replied that he had read the book and thanked Xiaoyu for reminding him of it. Xiaoyu asked questions about his horse and how it compared with the horse "Pilgrim." Was his horse superior and have a better understanding of human feelings? Hart said, "What is more important is that men to understand horses better, not the other way around. If we are to coexist with nature and animals in peace, we need to understand them and know how to communicate with them as equals."

Hart's perspective caught Xiaoyu's interest. They decided to start a one-on-one conversation outside of the chat room. Hart said his house was over 100 years old, frequented by skunks, spiders, lizards and geckos. Even squirrels and birds from the nearby forests would often come by unannounced. Hart called these animals the spirits of the old house. Xiaoyu told Hart that inside the stone gate housing of Shanghai where she lived there were also crickets, spiders and mosquitoes, as well as a mysterious green snake. Legend had it that spiders were the messengers for honored guests, and the snake was the guardian angel of the old house. She also advised him to check the Chinese legend about the white snake and the green snake on the Internet, as well as the rich cultural significance of the stone gate housing of Shanghai, a city of the Orient.

When Xiaoyu went offline that day, Renyan had already left and she wasn't even sure when he had gone. From then on, Renyan never set foot in Xiaoyu's garret apartment. Soon after, Xiaoyu learned from others that Renyan was now seeing a filing clerk who worked in the same company.

Xiaoyu and Hart became close friends on the Internet. They always met around midnight Beijing time. Xiaoyu opened her heart to Hart across the ocean. She needed a soul mate. The space-defying friendship had filled the emptiness left by the departure of Renyan.

They sometimes agreed to participate together in the wedding of a certain netizen on the Internet, or would watch the latest Hollywood movie together online that would share all the information about the movie, such as the private file of an actor or actress on the screen. Sometimes, they would tell to each other their latest find and most interesting websites. Later she came to understand how people, through messages, a news report, or lonely heart ads, could fall in love by the impact of two hearts clashing. Of course, it didn't necessarily mean that she and Hart would develop a relationship off line. Web friends are web friends. Their relationship is at once real and unreal, something that no actual relationship can replace.

Sometimes Xiaoyu would think of Renyan. She figured that he became interested in the other girl during the time when his visits became less frequent. Renyan also stopped trying to make out with her, and spent all of his time playing computer games and net surfing. By all accounts, he acted like a gentleman. Maybe he had tried to explain, but was at a loss of words. Slowly, Xiaoyu came to understand the situation from his perspective. He couldn't explain how their relationship fell apart, just like she couldn't explain how she found a soulmate in Hart.

Some of his things were still at Xiaoyu's place, like his computer. Although they lived in the same city, they seemed so far away from each other, and had stopped communicating with one another. Xiaoyu had thought of calling him, but soon had a change of heart. She figured that Renyan would certainly show up one day at her garret apartment and bade her goodbye. She understood later that there are certain things that are impossible to face or explain. When she realized this, she sent an email to Little Monkey in Bonn, which contained only two sentences: Renyan and I went our separate ways. You are a great Cassandra.

Xiaoyu moved out of the garret apartment not long afterwards. The crazy man whose wife disappeared in Japan had an episode one night. He walked aimlessly in the alleyway, pointing his fingers to the dark sky. He kept on saying, "The airplane is here, the airplane is here. I am about to board the plane! My wife is sending for me, I am going to Tokyo!"

The crazy man then threw small pebbles at her apartment window, saying that the window light had scared the plane away. That was the night Xiaoyu and Hart met in cyberspace. She couldn't sleep that night after the scare, and later moved out of Jiqing Li.

She gave Renyan's computer to Tianye. Like Renyan, she never set foot back there. She thought about the day she first set foot in Jiqing Li with Renyan from time to time. She could still see the rows of bamboo rods decorating the sky of the alleyway and the dripping washed clothes of all different colors hanging on them like wet sad faces. This narrow alleyway and its old stone gate housing infested with spiders and mosquitoes seemed to make an impact daily in her life. People would immediately recognize her as a standard Shanghai girl wherever she went. Once in Wolf Castle, Germany, she came across a Chinese restaurant owner, who with just one look at her and asked right away, "Are you from Shanghai? You must be!"

At the company's Chinese New Year party, someone came up with the idea of "picture showing." Everyone was asked to produce all the pictures they carried, be they picture of their wives, husbands, or lovers. Many married men couldn't produce pictures of their wives. They had all kinds of bankcards and VIP cards. Whereas the unmarried ones were able to show off the pictures of their loved ones treasured in their wallets or notebooks. Xiaoyu showed them the picture of Renyan, although they were no longer together at the time.

Xiaoyu noticed that Lenny was showing a picture of several

people, saying that the one she loved was one of the happy faces shown. Xiaoyu found the innocent face of Little Monkey in the picture. Xiaoyu flashed a knowing smile at Lenny and said nothing. At that moment, she felt she was lucky to have kept the picture of Renyan.

Stories by Contemporary Writers from Shanghai

A Pair of Jade Frogs
Ye Xin

Ah, Blue Bird
Lu Xing'er

Beautiful Days
Teng Xiaolan

Between Confidantes
Chen Danyan

Calling Back the Spirit of the Dead
Peng Ruigao

Dissipation
Tang Ying

Folk Song
Li Xiao

Forty Roses
Sun Yong

Game Point
Xiao Bai

Gone with the River Mist
Yao Emei

Goodby, Xu Hu!
Zhao Changtian

His One and Only
Wang Xiaoyu

Labyrinth of the Past
Zhang Yiwei

Memory and Oblivion
Wang Zhousheng

No Sail on the Western Sea
Ma Yuan

Normal People
Shen Shanzeng

Paradise on Earth
Zhu Lin

Platinum Passport
Zhu Xiaolin

River under the Eaves
Yin Huifen

She She
Zou Zou

The Confession of a Bear
Sun Wei

The Elephant
Chen Cun

The Little Restaurant
Wang Anyi

The Messenger's Letter
Sun Ganlu

The Most Beautiful Face in the World
Xue Shu

There Is No If
Su De

Vicissitudes of Life
Wang Xiaoying

When a Baby Is Born
Cheng Naishan

White Michelia
Pan Xiangli